Madeline -

Enjoy this story and remember Christmas of 2002 in Arizona + Disneyland (California).

We love you.

Grandpa + Grandma

Because of a Horse

To Madeline,
I hope you enjoy -
from Grandpa and
Grandma Amend

Darlene M Lawrence

11-8-02

Because of a Horse

A Novel

Darlene M. Lawrence

VANTAGE PRESS
New York

This is a work of fiction. Any similarity between the names, characters, and places in this book, and any persons, living or dead, is purely coincidental.

FIRST EDITION

Published by Vantage Press, Inc.
516 West 34th Street, New York, New York 10001

Manufactured in the United States of America
ISBN: 0-533-013911-2

Library of Congress Catalog Card No.: 01-126392

0 9 8 7 6 5 4 3 2 1

To my husband, BJ, my children, Valerie, Connie, Monica, and Bob, and to my sister, Marcia, for their encouragement, help, and just being who they are.

Because of a Horse

1

Christy Baldwin slowly rode her registered Arabian mare up the long winding drive of her parents' country estate. White board fences lined both sides of the drive, and emerald green meadows covered the rolling hills in the distance. A small yellow breasted meadowlark sat on the fence nearby, but its cheerful song couldn't change the bitter mood that had settled over the rider.

The doctor had been witty, but Christy couldn't recall any of his one-line jokes. He had said she was in perfect health, she had passed the examination with flying colors, so now she would be shipped off to a girl's school to learn proper etiquette, manners, dancing and dress. What a way to start high school!

"And how to serve tea!" she burst forth angrily, frightening the meadowlark from its lofty perch.

Victoree, the chestnut mare, turned one ear slightly backward, as she listened to the young rider. Christy patted the horse's arched neck and smoothed the long mane.

"Really, Victoree, what do I need all of that polish for? Mother thinks I'm a slob. She must anyway. Her and her family tree! Big deal. I won't see you until Thanksgiving or maybe not until Christmas! Skirts all the time and dressing for dinner. What for? What's wrong with school here?"

Victoree continued up the drive and stopped at

the stable gate. She waited for the slim fourteen year old girl to dismount. Christy, still mumbling to herself, slid gracefully from the horse's back. She pushed the latch upward, the gate swung open, and the horse and rider passed through.

"I know Rochester isn't Boston or a Southern plantation, but we have everything I want. I'll miss all my friends and you, Victoree. I won't even be here in January when you have your very first colt. Why must Mother be so hotse-totsi? I really don't care if Grandfather and Grandmother Mitchell came from a long line of blue-bloods. I'm just me!" Christy complained, slamming the gate behind them. A small black and white kitten scampered away, frightened by the sudden banging of the closing gate.

Christy led the mare inside the long, white horse barn. From the windows she could see the green landscaped lawn spreading across several acres, the two story brick house and rows of white fence. It looked more like a Southern mansion than a country home in southeastern Minnesota. In the distance, tree covered hills bathed with multicolored leaves ran a jagged line along the horizon. The fall colors would soon give way to winter white. The chill in the air promised an early frost, and the ice blue sky almost breathed the smell of snow.

Christy neither cared about or looked at the array of fall colors before her. She pushed the sliding door of the stable to one side and threw the reins over Victoree's neck. The horse entered as several horse heads appeared above the line of box stall doors. A

J. FLAGG

black Arabian stallion neighed a welcome from the stall at the far end. Christy patted each nose as she followed the chestnut mare to her stall. Once inside, Victoree turned and waited for the grain that she was sure to receive.

"Wait until I've unsaddled you," Christy said, pushing the mare's head to one side. "You also need a good rubdown. Don't be in such a rush."

Gathering brushes, combs, and a dampened sponge from the nearby tack room, Christy proceeded to spend as much time as possible cleaning the horse. Victoree's flaxen mane and tail glistened like copper as the late afternoon sun filtered through the window. The blaze on her face and her stocking legs were so white that the soft pink of the mare's skin showed through.

Christy dreaded the thought of entering the big house. How could she convince her parents that she wouldn't be happy in a Massachusetts girl's school? There was so little time left. Just a week and she would be boarding a plane at the Twin Cities International Airport.

2

Margaret Baldwin brushed an imaginary fleck of lint from her double-knit sports suit. The deep bronze color accented with a shaded orange, brown and gold neck scarf furnished Margaret with the look of elegance that she always strived to achieve. She glanced in the gold framed mirror as she placed the telephone receiver back in the cradle. Automatically, she straightened a strand of her dark auburn hair.

What business was it of a family doctor whether her only daughter wanted to attend a private school or not? He really didn't know very much about what Christina could or would learn there. He probably had spent his entire life west of the Mississippi River and had no idea of the finer things in life, she thought. Christina was certain to have some misgivings and be a little upset. This was all new to her, but once she got her mind off that silly horse and met some of the other girls at school, everything would be just fine.

Margaret hurried to pass her husband's study, hoping he hadn't heard the short telephone conversation.

"Who was that, Margaret?" Walter Baldwin asked, as he continued to read the list of figures before him.

"Oh, just Doctor Miller. He completed Christina's examination and she is in the best of health. He said I could pick up the forms tomorrow."

"Place isn't going to seem the same without her. Sure hate to see her go," Walter mumbled, turning to open another ledger.

"Yes, it will seem different," Margaret answered, trying to drop the conversation and move on past the open door.

Walt, as his close friends called him, pushed the book aside and raised his head. The blonde hair with slightly graying temples fell neatly into place as he looked at his slender wife. His deep blue eyes looked intensely into hers as if trying to find some hidden answer.

"Are you really so certain Christy will be happy there? She won't even discuss it and she's always been such a good student. Why take a chance and make her unhappy now? These schools were good enough for me, and by the time she's ready for college, she'll be old enough to choose where she wants to go."

"Oh, Walter, you are such a typical man! What's good enough for you and your father. Well, it's just not enough. Christina can't spend the rest of her life on the back of a horse! Why did you choose me? It certainly proves that you wanted someone with proper manners, someone who knows where to place the silver at a formal dinner and the ability to carry on an intelligent conversation."

"Okay, Margaret," Walt answered resignedly, as he thought back to their early courtship and marriage. "Only, I can't remember silver servings, formal dinners, or intelligent conversations having much to do with it," he muttered to himself, as he pictured long flowing auburn hair windblown across a smiling face as they ran hand in hand along a sandy beach.

Margaret sighed a breath of relief as she moved into the adjoining family room. She momentarily leaned on the arm of the overstuffed white leather sofa. As far as she was concerned, there had been enough discussion as to Christina going to a girl's school. There had been days when Walter appeared to be opposing the idea, and if he definitely decided against it, there would be no changing his mind. If only Christina didn't have this insane love for her horse. Margaret was determined. She would make a lady, not a cowgirl, of her daughter, her only child.

3

Christy was still lacing the front eyelets of her clean soft blue shorts as she hurried into the dining room.

"You are rather late, dear, and you really should have put on some slacks. The air is cool," Margaret said, as she poured tall glasses of ice tea. "We were about to eat without you."

"I'm sorry, Mother," Christy replied, "I was cleaning my saddle."

"You are always cleaning your saddle, or your horse, or the tack room, or something in that barn. I wish you would spend part of your time reading, creating a new hobby, or something beneficial. I'll be so happy when you learn and become fascinated with some of the subjects you will have in school.

"I remember studying French," Margaret went on. "We even dressed in authentic French clothing and attended classes as young mademoiselles. How we enjoyed it!"

"I'm sure you did," Christy answered, in a sarcastic tone. She quickly busied herself with the food before her as she noticed her father lay his fork beside his plate.

"Perhaps this Eastern education is what you need, Christy. That is no tone of voice to use while speaking to your mother."

Walter Baldwin's steel-blue eyes looked intensely at his daughter, and his German ancestry showed in the firm line of his jaw. Christy knew better than to speak.

Margaret quickly changed the subject and repeated the neighborhood small talk of her latest bridge game. The awkward conversation was finally broken when the gardener drove his blue pickup into the yard.

"You'd think he'd know when people ate around here," Walt grumbled, as he left the room.

"I'm sorry, Christina," Margaret said, sweetly. "I didn't mean to upset you or your father. I know you are a little frightened about going so far from home. The time will fly, and you'll be home for Thanksgiving in just three months."

Christy looked at her mother and her blue green eyes filled with tears. Why, her mother wasn't even looking in her direction. She was idly sipping her iced tea as she watched the men outside.

"Oh, dear. It looks as if they are coming inside. Hurry, Christina, help me clear these dishes!"

4

Christy had excused herself as quickly as possible. She was about to go up the stairs to her bedroom when she overheard a bit of her parent's conversation. They were talking about the doctors' convention at which Walter would speak. Christy had been so preoccupied with her own problems she had completely forgotten that her parents would be leaving late Wednesday afternoon and would not return until early Sunday morning. She was to stay with her Aunt Loretta.

"At least it will be a lot better than staying here," Christy whispered to herself, as she climbed the open stairway. "I know Aunt Lettie will let me ride Victoree over to her place, and I can keep her there until I have to come home."

Once again Christy's eyes filled with tears as she entered her bedroom. As soon as she closed the door behind her, she let the tears flow. Uncontrollable sobs rushed to the surface. Christy threw herself on her lavender-and-white canopied bed, quickly grabbing a large soft pillow to muffle the sounds of her heartbroken cry.

It was an hour or so later when Margaret knocked on Christy's door.

"Your father and I are having a little bedtime snack," Margaret said. "Would you like to have some ice cream or something else and join us?"

"No, Mother, I'm getting ready for bed and I want to write a few letters with my new address. I want to get some mail as soon as I can."

"That's a great idea, Christina," Margaret replied. "You'll have so much to write about, and I know your friends will be so anxious to hear from you. Goodnight, dear, we'll see you in the morning."

Christy got up and looked in the mirror above her white and gold dresser. Her eyes were red and swollen; her nose was an even brighter red. Her long auburn hair hung in large wet strands from the tears that had overwhelmed her. Slowly the hot coals of anger began to fill her body.

"I'm not going! I don't know how, but I'm not going," Christy said angrily. "I'm just not going to go!"

The stars were shining brightly, and a crescent moon cast shadows around the trees and fences below. Christy, unable to sleep, sat by her open window and let the cold night air cool the anger within her. She knew the only way she could keep from boarding that airplane on Monday was to disappear—to run away. But how, without being found, in an area where she and Victoree were so well known? Of course, she would take Victoree. She would go somewhere, someplace—a place that she could be with her beautiful mare. And, in January, be with her when the little baby colt was born.

Christy had no idea that the plans she was making would change her life forever.

5

"Christina, it's time for your breakfast. Better hurry! I want to do some shopping for school clothes today. I also want to see about a new banquet dress for your dad's convention. He is one of the speakers, you know," Margaret said, as she put Walter's coffee cup into the dishwasher.

"Be right down, Mother. I just have to brush my hair," Christy answered, trying to sound as nonchalant as possible. "What time will we get home?"

"Oh, by 3:30 or 4 o'clock," Margaret replied. "You'll have plenty of time to ride your horse."

"Thanks, Mother. I really want to ride today," Christy responded, as she hurried to the breakfast table. She quickly poured milk on her cereal and began to eat. She was so conscious of the slight quiver in her voice and only hoped her mother wouldn't notice.

"I'll dash up and get ready, dear. Will you stick your dishes in the washer?" Margaret asked as she wiped the counter and placed the milk carton back in the refrigerator.

"Sure," Christy said, busily turning the pages of the morning newspaper to the cartoons.

The young girl sighed with relief when her mother left the room. She knew it was going to be difficult to appear as if everything were okay and that she was planning on going to the Boston school. Her heart felt like it was thumping out of control, and there was a lump in her throat that seemed to get larger by the minute.

The telephone rang and Christy could hear her mother's muffled voice coming from the master bedroom. Soon Margaret entered the kitchen.

"Aunt Loretta wants to go with us, and I would appreciate her input on what dress I should buy. You don't mind, do you, dear?" Margaret asked.

"No, that's great. She can even help pick out my clothes," Christy answered, folding the newspaper. Another little sigh of relief escaped Christy's lips as she pictured Aunt Lettie seated in the front seat, chatting with her mother. This would allow Christy to be in the back. She would try to act natural, try not to cry and even work at showing some interest in the clothes they would buy.

The day passed quickly, and much was said with oohs and aahs as the saleslady brought sweaters, skirts, jackets, and several dresses for Christy to try on. Later, loaded with packages and not one but two evening dresses for Margaret, the trio returned to the Baldwin estate. The plans had been reviewed over lunch for Christy to stay with Loretta while the Baldwins were out of town. Christy quickly took her new clothes to her bedroom to hang and put away. She could hardly wait to change clothes and go to the stable.

"Victoree, I'm so glad to finally get here," Christy

said, as the mare softly nickered when the young girl opened the door. "Only two more days and we'll be together all the time. I wish it was today."

Christy brushed, bridled, and saddled the mare. Only a few minutes had passed and the graceful mare with a determined young rider cantered down the long driveway. The yellow-breasted meadowlark sang one more song and then flew away as the girl and horse turned onto the road.

"We'll look for a place to get into the woods, someplace where no one is close enough to notice. When we leave we'll have to head south. I'm not sure where we'll go, just as far away as possible," the girl said, holding back tears as she patted the arched neck of the Arabian mare. Flicking one ear back to listen to the rider, the copper colored horse pulled at the bridle bit and increased her speed.

"Easy, Victoree, you can't wear yourself out today. We'll go to Aunt Lettie's tomorrow, stay there overnight, and Thursday be on our way. Just you and I, girl, just you and I."

FLAGG

6

Wednesday morning dawned with heavy clouds and a weather forecast stating there would be light showers off and on in the afternoon.

"Hurry," Margaret called to Christy. "Your father is taking the suitcases out, and Aunt Loretta is driving up the lane. We can't be late."

"I'm coming, Mother," Christy answered. She quickly slipped into a denim jacket and hurried down the stairs.

Walt had the suitcases in the trunk of his sister's car as Margaret and Christy crawled into the back seat.

"Looks like rain," Walt said, as he slid into the seat next to his sister. "Thanks for taking us to the airport, Lettie, and for taking care of my girl for the weekend," he added, as he turned and smiled at Christy. "You be a good girl, and don't give your aunt any problems."

Christy swallowed hard and held back the tears that were about to overflow.

"You know she'll be just fine," Lettie replied. "I'll take her back to the house, and she can ride Victoree over to my place. We'll ride until we can't ride anymore. I haven't had Bandana out nearly enough lately. That old gelding will be getting soft if I don't ride him more often."

Christy forced a smile and agreed they would

have a great time. It was becoming more and more difficult to keep from giving her secret away. She weighed every word to make sure she would not slip and make her parents suspicious.

"What's my big brother going to speak on this time?" Lettie asked. "Some great medical breakthrough you've kept from us until you could spring it on your audience?"

"No, Sis," Walt responded. "It's on the health care issue. It's getting to be quite a problem."

"Well, get it all straightened out before I need it," Lettie said. "Are they having a lot of things for the women to do, Margaret?"

"Oh, yes. We're going to tour some of the old Twin City mansions, have a Fall Style Show with our ladies luncheon. Lots of things and I want to do some shopping," Margaret answered.

At last they were at the airport. The wait to board the plane would be short. Christy hated to think of the good-byes that had to be said, and she tried not to think about not being able to see her parents again for a long time. She did love them, but she couldn't understand why they didn't know how she felt. She just couldn't go to some far off place and leave Victoree behind.

"They are calling our flight, Walter," Margaret said. "Christina, come give your mother and dad a kiss good-bye."

Christy pecked her mother softly on the cheek and was about to turn to her dad when Margaret put her arms around Christy and hugged her daughter tightly. Tears started to flow down Christy's cheeks as her dad reached and pulled her into his arms.

"Now, now, Christy. We won't be gone that long, and we'll still have a day or so before you leave. I'll tell you what. When we get back, I'll saddle up Black Destiny and we'll go for a long ride. You and Victoree will have a hard time keeping up," Walt said, as he gave his daughter an extra squeeze.

"I don't think so, Dad," Christy said, then remembering to keep her plans a secret, she added, "Victoree's pretty fast." She forced a smile to appear on her face and wiped the tears that were still forming and running down her cheeks.

"We'll see about that," Walt responded, as he gave Lettie a quick hug. "See you real soon."

The good-byes were said. Christy and her Aunt Lettie drove back to the Baldwins' home.

"Do you want me to help you get some things together, dear?" Lettie asked.

"No, I'll just grab some pj's and a couple of things. I'll stick them in my saddle bags and come across the north pasture, it's a lot shorter. See you pretty soon," Christy answered, turning quickly to keep Lettie from seeing her face.

"Okay, honey. I'm going to stop at the store and pick up a few things. Won't take but a few minutes."

"Okay, bye," Christy replied.

7

Christy hurried into the house and was about to change into a pair of jeans and her riding boots when the telephone rang. It was her best friend, Jennifer Williams.

"Hi, Christy. Did your parents leave?" Jenny asked.

"Yes, I just got back from the airport. Why?" Christy replied, pulling her jeans from the drawer.

"Barb is coming over Friday night, and we thought you should come too. It will be our last chance before you leave for Boston. Remember the last time we three stayed over at Barb's? We hardly slept all night! What a night that was. My sides ached from laughing for days. Barb said there are a couple of new guys in our class this year. She'll give us the latest. She did say they are pretty cool."

"I'll have to ask my aunt," Christy answered. "I'm staying at her place while Mother and Dad are gone. It sounds great."

"Are you okay, Christy?" Jennifer questioned. "You don't sound like yourself. Is everything all right?"

"I'm fine. I was just changing clothes and going to ride Victoree over to my aunt's. I better hurry or she'll wonder what happened to me. I'm sure it will be okay with her. Hey, just plan on me coming. If she won't let me, I'll call you back. What time should I be there?" Christy responded, trying to sound excited about the sleepover.

"Come early. Say 3:30 or 4 o'clock. We'll pig out, play videos, whatever. If it warms up, we'll even take a swim in the pool."

"We'll have a blast. I better get going. See you Friday unless I call you back," Christy replied.

Christy hung up the phone and changed into her jeans and a light pink pullover.

"I won't even be here," she muttered to herself. "But I couldn't tell her, even if she is my best friend. I just can't let anyone know. I wish Victoree and I were already gone!"

Christy glanced at the phone as she pulled her riding boots on. A new plan began forming in her mind. She lifted the phone from its cradle and slowly dialed Aunt Lettie's number.

"Hello," Lettie said on the second ring.

"Hi, Aunt Lettie," Christy said. "I just got a call from Jennifer Williams. Remember her? I know you met her once when she was here. Anyway, she wants me to come and stay overnight. She said it was our last chance and Barbara Johnson is coming too. I know you know who she is. She's the blonde who's in my Sunday School class. You know her parents, don't you? I really want to go and I know Mother would let me. Please?"

"Oh, I don't know, Christy. I hardly know Jennifer and I don't know her folks at all. Are you sure they will be home?" Loretta asked.

"They'll be home. Dad works with Doctor Williams and Mrs. Williams is a good friend of Mother's. They even play bridge together all the time. Please let me go, Aunt Lettie. I'll be over to your house by 4:30 tomorrow," Christy begged. "It's my last chance for the three of us to be together, and they are my best friends."

"Oh—all right, Christy," Loretta responded. "But you give me Jennifer's telephone number. I'll be over to drive you."

Christy's heart seemed to skip a beat as she answered Loretta.

"They are coming to pick me up, Jennifer and Mrs. Williams. I told them I would call right back if it wasn't okay with you. Thanks loads, Aunt Lettie. I really appreciate it. See you tomorrow. Oh, and Jennifer's number is 383-5824."

Christy felt a twinge of guilt as she hung up the phone. She had lied to both Aunt Lettie and to Jennifer, and even transposed the last two numbers in Jennifer's telephone number. She hoped it would give her enough time to disappear.

Christy quickly stuffed another pair of jeans, a couple of shirts, socks, and whatever else she could into a small bag. She dumped the little bit of money that she had into her jean pocket and pulled a winter jacket and her rain slicker from the closet. At the last minute, she grabbed her hair brush, a bar of soap, and a towel. Once downstairs, she pulled a grocery bag out and filled it with some lunch meat, crackers, cheese, cookies, potato chips, candy, and some fruit.

"That should keep me going," she mumbled. "Oh, I better get a blanket."

Victoree whinnied softly as Christy entered the barn. The mare was anxiously waiting for her daily ride and the serving of grain that always followed.

"We're leaving, pretty girl. Right now," Christy said, as she quickly brushed and saddled her horse. She opened both saddle bags, filling one with grain for Victoree and the other with the food for herself. She then laid out the slicker and placed the clothes, blanket, and the other small items inside. Trembling, she rolled them tightly into a bundle and tied them onto the back of her western saddle. Then she took the canteen and lariat from her Dad's saddle. After filling the canteen with fresh water, she hung the strap over the saddle horn and tied the lariat securely in place.

As Christy rode Victoree down the long drive, a few sprinkles of rain began to fall. The horse and rider turned south.

"Take it easy, Victoree. We have a long way to go," Christy said.

8

Christy rode Victoree in amongst several groves of trees whenever possible. The fall foliage was brilliant—reds, yellows, golds, and greens. The young girl neither looked at nor cared about the beauty of the season. She was completely absorbed in carrying out her plans to get away. She had ridden only a few hours when she found a small stream. After Victoree had her fill of fresh water, they proceeded down stream making sure the hoofprints were washed away. A short time later it began to rain. The hoofprints that had remained on the roads, fields, and river bank disappeared from view.

Christy wished she had brought some plastic or something waterproof. Her slicker was wrapped around her blanket and extra clothes. She decided since she was already wet, she would leave her slicker rolled up and keep her blanket and the rest of her clothes dry.

Chilled and dripping wet, the young rider urged the horse into a brisk trot. They kept moving through the night. Victoree would often shake her head. The rain in her ears and running down her face was something that she seldom had to contend with.

"I know, Victoree. You Arabians aren't much for water, are you? It took forever to get you to cross a stream or even step in a puddle. It's a good thing you are finally over that," Christy said. "It will be a long night, girl. Maybe it will stop raining tomorrow. I hope so."

At last the first rays of dawn tried to break through the dark, heavy clouds to the east. Christy started to look for a safe place to hide and rest. "We've got to stay out of sight during the day, Victoree. I'm sure we are already in hot water. I hope Aunt Lettie doesn't try that phone number! She doesn't get upset very often. I hate to put her through all of this. She's always been so good to me. Even stuck up for me when I've been in trouble with Mother," Christy continued. "I wish I'd brought a road map. I think that was Spring Valley back there where we saw those lights. Might have been some other town, I'm not sure. We must be close to the Iowa line."

In the distance loomed a large stack of baled hay. The cattle must have broken through the fence around it, as the one side of the stack had some broken bales and several were lying in a large pile.

"It's a perfect hide-out, Victoree. Let's go!"

They raced to the fence and found a gate. Christy dismounted and led her horse inside the enclosure. She then arranged some bales for a good wind break. They were at the far side of the stack, which protected them from the rain that was still coming down. It also shielded them from being seen from the road.

A herd of black and white Holstein cattle, grazing in a nearby pasture, watched as the girl unsaddled the mare, measured a short ration of grain, and pulled some hay loose for the tired horse. When she was sure that Victoree was taken care of, she changed into her dry clothes. She quickly dug out a few potato chips and an apple for herself. Exhausted, she folded the blanket in half and crawled between the two layers. Within minutes she was sound asleep.

The cattle, losing interest in the girl and horse, returned to graze the lush pasture. Day followed dawn as the farmer opened the big doors of the white dairy barn. The cows quickened their step and soon disappeared inside.

9

Loretta Martin had waited until almost five o'clock before she tried calling the Baldwin residence or the phone number Christy had given her. She had reasoned that Christy had a habit of being a little late, even to the dinner table, Margaret had often said. No one answered either number, so Loretta drove to the Baldwin estate. The hired man had been there and fed the horses. Victoree was gone.

Loretta pondered what that could mean. Christy had said the Williamses were picking her up yesterday. Maybe they were late getting her back and she was now riding to Loretta's home. Loretta decided the best thing to do would be to go back home to see if Christy had arrived.

Again, Loretta waited a short time before she dialed the Johnsons' residence and asked to speak to Barbara.

"Hello, this is Barbara."

"Barbara, this is Loretta Martin, Christy's aunt. I understand she was to be with you and Jennifer at Jennifer's home last night. She said she would be at my home by 4:30 this afternoon. Have you any idea where she is?" Loretta asked.

"Oh, Mrs. Martin. You must have misunderstood. We are staying at Jennifer's house on Friday night. I can hardly wait. The three of us are such good friends," Barbara replied.

"Oh, I see. Do you have Jennifer's number? Maybe Christy rode over there before coming to my house. I'll check with her," Loretta said, as she thought about her last conversation with Christy.

"Yes, Mrs. Martin. It is 383-5842. I hope everything is okay," Barbara answered.

"I'm sure it is. Just got our wires crossed, I guess," Loretta said, anxious to finish the conversation and call Jennifer. It was getting quite dark outside.

Loretta Martin, a tall, self-sufficient woman, was a kind and generous person. She never had any children of her own, Christy was the closest thing to a daughter she ever had. Loretta had lost her husband to cancer twelve years ago and had never found anyone to replace him. She was an attractive woman, slender, ash blonde hair and emerald blue eyes similar to her brother's. Only his could turn to steel blue if he was angered.

Loretta's hand was trembling as she picked up the phone and called the Williams' residence.

"Hello, this is Jennifer speaking."

A bit surprised and caught off guard, Loretta said, "This is Loretta Martin, Christina's aunt. Is she there?"

"Why, no, Mrs. Martin. I haven't seen her. She said she would come to my sleep-over Friday night when I talked to her yesterday. Is something wrong?" Jennifer questioned.

"Probably not. We just missed our connections, I guess. Thank you," Loretta answered.

"Mrs. Martin, Christy said she was riding her horse to your place yesterday. She said she had to hurry or you would be worried. Didn't she come?" Jennifer asked.

"No, she didn't. Don't worry. I'm sure there's an answer and everything will be fine," Loretta responded.

"Please let me know. Have Christy call me. Okay? I'll be so worried."

"I'll tell her to call. Thanks, Jennifer," Loretta said.

Loretta, now visibly shaken, tried to make some sense out of what was going on.

"If only I would have had some children of my own. Maybe then I could understand. What could have happened to Christy? Has someone abducted her? Wouldn't Victoree come home? Why wouldn't Christy just gallop away if there was a problem? I've got to call Walt and Margaret."

Margaret received the urgent message as she sat listening to her husband's intriguing speech. He noticed her leave the room and momentarily wondered why she had left. When he had finished his oration and returned to his seat at the head table, he was handed a note. He immediately excused himself and hurried to his hotel room.

Margaret met him at the door, sobbing that Christina was gone, lost, abducted. No one could find her.

Walt held his wife and tried to calm her to learn the whole confusing story. A return call to Loretta confirmed the worst. Christy was missing.

10

Christy kept Victoree well hidden from the farm nearby and from the road that ran near the buildings. She waited, which seemed like forever for the sun to go down. She noticed a pond in one of the fields a short distance away and knew Victoree needed a drink of water.

"As soon as it gets dark, we'll go there, good girl. I'm sorry we have to hide like this. It'll get better, I promise. If Mother and Dad couldn't get a plane last night, they'll be flying home today. They're probably already there."

Again the big barn doors opened and the dairy cattle went inside. The minutes continued to drag by. At last lights dotted the countryside showing where the neighborhood farms were located. All was quiet except for a dog barking in the farmer's yard. Finally, Christy felt it was safe to leave. This time she wore her slicker. Victoree tossed her head as the raindrops again hit her face. After closing the gate, Christy climbed into the saddle and reined the horse toward the pond she had seen. Victoree drank thirstily. Then the two headed for the country road.

"I guess we are ready, pretty girl," Christy murmured as she patted the mare's wet neck. "I'm glad it's raining to cover our tracks, but I sure hope it quits tomorrow. I wonder where we'll be by morning?"

Christy looked for a crossroad that was not traveled a lot. She crossed over a couple of roads that were streaming with traffic; she would hold Victoree back in the shadows until they could cross without being seen. Then she would urge Victoree into a fast trot, and they would disappear into the dark, rainy night on the other side.

Finally she found an old roadway that was used so seldom that grass had grown between the two tire tracks. She soon crossed a bridge that creaked with every step Victoree took, and then the winding road passed through a large grove of overhanging trees. Both Christy and Victoree jumped when what must have been an owl flew from its perch in a nearby tree. It was so close that it nearly touched them as it passed by. Another mile and they were back in clear country, much to the relief of the spooked, young girl.

The old road came to an end at another busy two lane highway. In the late night hours, there were only two cars in sight and after they had passed, Christy hesitated and wondered if she should turn right or left. When Victoree tried to turn to the left, Christy turned her to the right.

"You want to go home, don't you, Victoree?" the girl asked. "We can't do that. I can't take you back, pretty girl. Mother would probably talk Dad into taking you away from me. I would never see you again. I couldn't stand that. Come on, we've got to keep going. And I don't want to go to any girl's school!"

Just then a car topped the hill in front of them. Christy felt her heart skip a beat as she frantically looked for an escape route from the bright lights coming toward her. She quickly turned Victoree around, gave the horse a loose rein and pushed her mount into a full gallop. When they came to the old road, she turned the mare back the same way they had just traveled. When the car slowed down and turned the same corner, Christy was certain the driver had clearly seen her. She was positive the car was following her.

Victoree was a well-trained horse. She responded extremely well to each signal or cue that was given by her rider. The horse had been trained in jumping but had only been asked to jump over low obstacles or a few low fences in a trail class. Sometimes there would be a small stream. Victoree had always cleared them with at least a couple of feet to spare.

Christy had never ridden in a real jumping class. Her father felt she might get careless and get hurt. Fences, hedges, and ditches were all off limits. Of course, Christy had secretly jumped Victoree over some small ditches and some fallen logs in the woods near her home, but never a fence.

Now there was no choice. With a lump in her throat, Christy turned Victoree toward the old wooden fence beside the road. With a squeeze of the rider's knees and a slight lift of the reins, the mare gracefully cleared the fence and continued to gallop across the field.

Christy felt an empty sensation in her stomach, as if she were on a Ferris wheel as it came down from

J. FLAGG

the very top. She looked back and saw that the car was going down the old road.

"I guess they weren't chasing us after all. I just hope they didn't see us," Christy stammered as she slowed Victoree to a walk. "I was never so scared, and it was so hard to see where we were going. You must have better eyes than I do, pretty girl. Take it easy; you are sweating and you've got to cool down. You are a wonderful horse, Victoree, I would just die if anything happened to you or someone took you away from me. It won't be long and we'll find a place to stop. You really deserve your grain today!"

Something was moving in the field in front of them. Again the lump filled Christy's throat as she slowed Victoree and peered into the darkness. A chill ran up her spine as scary thoughts of an angry bull or a mean stallion crossed her mind. She knew better than to turn Victoree and run. That would only cause either of them to charge.

A flock of sheep! What a relief. The ewes with their half-grown lambs parted and let the horse and rider go on past. Then the whole flock turned and followed. A few streaks of dawn were coming over the horizon when Christy saw the sheep shed.

"We'll stay here today, Victoree. There's lots of grass. As soon as I get you unsaddled and brushed down, I'll take you out to graze. You are lucky to have all this food at your feet. I haven't got much left."

The sheep scattered when Christy led her horse from the three-sided shed. As the early dawn burst with sunshine, Christy knew the rain was over. She led Victoree to a water tank close by. After a long drink, Victoree was once again well taken care of. They hid in the sheep shed, and again the tired horse and rider had a place to rest and sleep.

11

Christy led Victoree out of the sheep shed as soon as darkness fell. Victoree had not been too happy to share the building with so many furry animals. Christy had to keep herding them to the far end of the shed. Finally the flock had gone out to pasture to graze. Christy had laid her clothes out and was able to dry them in the warmth of the day.

She ate a few cookies before getting ready for the long night ride. She tried to make the food last as long as possible, but hunger pains convinced her to eat her last apple. She would have to buy some food no later than the next day. There were only two more feedings of grain for Victoree. She pulled the money that she had from her jean pocket. Twenty-six dollars and fifty cents. Not much but she would find somewhere to buy grain and maybe some rolls and dried fruit. She filled her canteen with fresh water from the pump as Victoree drank from the water tank. They were ready to go.

The country roads were dark and deserted as the horse and rider rode through the night. High yellowing corn fields lined the roadways on both sides. Now and then a corn picker stood idle in a half picked field. The grain fields that she passed were just stubble. The oats had been combined a few weeks earlier. It was fall, harvest time.

"This is our third day out, Victoree," Christy said

to her horse. "I'm not sure what to do but I'll take care of you. If we can get far enough away and maybe if I dye my hair, I can work on a farm or something. They'll have our pictures all over TV and everything. I'll think of something."

Christy was now almost sixty-eight miles south of her home. She was in a large farming community in Iowa. Here and there Victoree's hoofprints could be spotted along the dusty road, but it seemed unlikely anyone would be looking for her in this area.

Christy couldn't believe it when Victoree just stopped and tried to eat. Then she saw the oats on the ground. A wagon must have been too full and lost part of its load as it pulled up the embankment onto the road. The farmer must have thought there was not enough there to be worth picking up. Christy slid from the saddle and filled the one saddle bag to overflowing. She let Victoree eat what she figured would be a good feeding and then pulled her away.

"That was wonderful, pretty girl," Christy said, smiling for the first time in quite a while. "Let's keep going. If we can be so lucky now as to find a store, we'll both be in good shape for a few days."

It was close to 10:30 P.M. when they came to a paved highway. Off to the right and about a quarter of a mile away, the highway intersected with another blacktop road. There on the corner stood a gas station with neon lights. It was still open.

Christy reined Victoree down into the ditch that ran along the highway. Several cars whizzed by, and a semi truck pulled into the station as Christy and Victoree went behind the building.

Her heart felt as if it would pound its way out of her body as Christy dismounted and pulled her money out of her pocket. She stayed in the shadows until she was near the entrance. The clerk and the truck driver were discussing the weather and things in general while Christy hurriedly picked up some candy bars, crackers spread with cheese, a small package of doughnuts, even a Coke, and as she moved to the counter, she saw a large package of trail mix.

The clerk, an elderly gentleman, rang up the total.

"That will be $8.95, Miss. Haven't seen you around here before. Where are you from?" he asked.

"We're just passing through. Heading south for the winter," Christy answered. She hoped he thought she was a passenger in a car. She tried to keep her head down as she picked up the change.

"Hey, look at that," the truck driver said, as he watched the late news on the television above the counter. "That doctor in Rochester is putting up a $50,000 reward for his fourteen-year-old daughter. Wonder what happened to her?"

"Can't find hide nor hair of her from what's on the news. I guess her . . ." That was all Christy heard as she went through the door. She felt sick to her stomach and for the first time wished she was safe at home.

Christy stuffed the sack of food into the saddle

bag and reined Victoree into the darkness. The soft sound of hoofbeats racing across the grass was not heard as the cars sped by. Once again, the old country road was the safest haven to travel. Christy turned Victoree back the way they had come.

"We have to find our way home, Victoree. We can't let anyone find us. I don't want Dad to pay that reward. I'm so scared," Christy cried.

The truck driver left the station after the weather report. Good weather all the way through Nebraska. He would get home tomorrow night. He switched on the radio as he circled the station to turn his truck around. As the bright lights from his truck hit the hoofprints where Victoree had been tied, the picture of the girl on the news flashed through his mind. He slammed on the brakes and pulled the truck out of gear; he jumped out and raced back inside the station.

"Hey, that girl that was just in here. She rode off on a horse. I'll bet it's that missing girl. I can't chase her down with my truck. Call the highway patrol. Hurry. Let me talk to them."

Christy was now deep in a cornfield. She had taken the time to brush all the hoofprints away when she left the road. Deep prints showed in the cornfield. She only hoped it would be a day or so before anyone found the tracks.

Christy had no idea the highway patrol was already searching the area.

12

Christy and Victoree had spent the night traveling through corn fields higher than her head, sometimes across a pasture or a stubbled field where grain had once grown. The girl and her horse often had to circle inside the fence line until they found a gate to go through. They had come out of the fields to cross a country road and then entered into more fields on the other side. The big, damp leaves, now covered with early morning dew, slapped the girl and horse, sometimes even across Christy's face when she could not catch them in time.

"You hate this, don't you, Victoree?" Christy asked. "I'm so sorry I got you into this. Even if I had to go to that old school, you would be okay. I just hope we can get home. I'm not even sure how to get there anymore. Mother is probably sick; you know how things upset her. And, Dad, he's probably really worried but won't let it show. And poor Aunt Lettie. She must feel terrible. I still don't want to go to that girl's school, but I sure messed things up. Fifty thousand dollars! We've got to find our way home on our own."

Christy stopped Victoree in the edge of a corn field when they came to another road. It was a dirt road, almost like a farmer's field road. Christy looked both ways and was about to go through the open gate. The sound of a motor close by caused her to pull Victoree back into the tall corn stalks. Christy parted the heavy leaves as the car went by. A highway patrol! The patrolman had to be looking for her! It was getting light out, but they had to move on. It was only a matter of time until someone found their tracks. When the patrol car rounded the corner, Christy leaped on Victoree and sped across the road. There was not time to brush hoofprints off the road. Now there was only a little time until the uniformed men would find signs of the horse and rider.

As Christy and Victoree passed through another corn field, they came upon an open field that led them toward a small hill. Christy could see a few trees dotting the hillside. A windmill pumped water into a tank and a herd of white-faced Hereford cattle lay under the trees as they chewed their cud. Christy slowed Victoree to a walk. She did not want to scare the cattle, but she had to get Victoree to the water. It had been a long time since the mare had had a drink. Some of the cattle got up as horse and rider moved closer, but they did not scatter. Christy looked for a bull among them, but it was the wrong time of the year for the animal to be out with the cows.

Christy dismounted at the water tank and splashed cold water across her face as Victoree drank her fill. The refreshing water softened the tightness of her skin and washed the tear stained streaks from her cheeks.

"I've got to let you rest, Victoree, but we can't stop yet. Here, let me pull the bridle bit from your mouth and you can eat a little grass. These red cows around us pretty much hide us from view. You're not the same color, but kind of," Christy said, as she led her horse to where some of the herd was busy munching on the grass.

As the cattle moved over the top of the hill, Christy kept Victoree with them. Another patrol car slowly passed on the road below. Christy ducked among the cattle. She hoped Victoree would not raise her head till the car was gone.

Once out of sight, Christy tightened the cinch on her saddle and put the bit back in the horse's mouth. As quickly as possible, she mounted her horse and galloped to the gate below. She dismounted, opened and then closed the gate so the cattle could not get out. She could see the crossroad to the left. Just as she was getting back in the saddle, she saw a large, white, enclosed truck turning onto the road in front of her. There was no time to open and close the gate.

Christy urged Victoree to jump, but the horse knew the gate was too high. Victoree swerved to the right, and Christy fell from the saddle. The truck screeched to a halt.

"It's okay. We know who you are. Don't be scared," a young woman called, as she and a man rushed from the truck. "Where are you going? Are you okay?"

"I'm okay," Christy answered, as she sat up in the deep grass. Victoree stood nearby. The young man picked up the reins and led Victoree back to Christy.

"I want to go home. I ran away, and I'm so sorry," Christy said, as she burst into tears.

"There, there. Everything is going to be all right. We'll take you home. My name is Sally, and you are Christina. Right?" the young woman asked.

"Here, let's put your horse in the truck and get going," the dark-haired man said. "There's cops all over the place looking for you."

"I know. I've seen them," Christy said. "Will you really take me home?"

"Of course we will," Sally answered. "This is my husband, Bill. Now hurry. We better get going if we are going to make it to Rochester by tonight. Oh, we have a big Collie dog. Will your horse ride with him if we put him in the back?"

"I don't know," Christy responded. "Why don't I ride in back with Victoree? I have a blanket and could lie down. I'm so tired."

"That would be just fine if that is what you want to do," Sally said. "Old Duke is used to riding up front with us anyway. In you go."

The truck started down the old country road. Christy was exhausted. The purr of the motor and the slight rumble of the tires below were like music to Christy's ears.

"We're going home, Victoree," she mumbled, as she drifted off to sleep.

13

Christy woke up when the truck stopped at a filling station. Sally pushed the small window behind the cab of the truck open.

"Be real quiet, Christy. We don't want anyone to know you are with us. They'd call the cops," Sally said. "I'm going in and get you a hamburger, french fries, and a Coke. I'll bet you are really hungry. Old Duke will keep everyone away from the truck."

"Thanks," Christy mumbled. "I am hungry."

When the truck pulled out of the station and Sally passed the food through the little window, Christy asked how long before they would be in Rochester.

"Probably three or four hours," Bill answered, gruffly. "Just relax."

"Just rest, Christy. You must be awfully tired. You've had a long ride," Sally said. "I'll close the window so our talking doesn't keep you awake."

Christy lay back on her blanket after eating everything she had been given.

"It's still a long ride, Victoree. I had no idea we had come so far," she sleepily muttered.

Christy awoke with a start as she noticed that it was pitch black outside and the truck was again pulling into a gas station. This time the window was opened only a crack.

"Be absolutely quiet," Bill commanded. "Make a noise and you'll never see your mother or dad again."

"Why? What do you mean?" Christy stammered.

"Just shut up!" Bill answered, as he got out of the truck.

"Be good, Christy," Sally said, in a whisper. "Bill has a bad temper and is tired."

"Are we almost to my house?" Christy asked, in a low whisper.

"Shhhh. Here he comes," Sally responded, as she closed the window.

Fear gripped Christy as she moved back from the window. Where were they taking her? Was it the reward money that they were after?

The hours passed slowly as they traveled on down the long highway. Christy fed Victoree some grain and wished she had some hay and water for her.

Finally the truck pulled over, but Christy couldn't see anything in the darkness ahead. One side of the back double doors opened slightly, and Bill threw in a bale of hay.

"That old farmer won't miss a bale, and I don't want a dead horse on my hands," Christy heard Bill say.

"We'll have to get a pail and some water," Sally answered.

"Later. Let's get going," Bill replied. "We've got to get out of this part of the country in a hurry. They'll be stopping every truck before too long."

Panic stricken, Christy realized they weren't

taking her to Rochester. She had been kidnaped. They weren't after the $50,000 reward money. They were after much, much more.

14

Two days passed as they continued traveling, sometimes on an interstate, sometimes along a two-lane highway. Either Sally or Bill stayed in the truck at all times. The hamburgers and breakfast rolls that they brought Christy now tasted like sawdust. She could hardly swallow. Her throat and mouth felt swollen and dry. Only the milk, Coke, or water they sometimes gave her seemed to help.

The couple had passed a pail of water into the back of the truck several times for Victoree. The horse was content, relaxed and rested. Christy hardly slept.

Christy had not been able to see anything the few times the door had been slightly opened. Bill had told her to stay back, and she had done exactly what he said. She was deathly afraid of him. Even Sally was no longer friendly. The huge dog always sat between them and Christy was too panic stricken to get close to the window. She had no idea where they were.

At last the truck turned onto a gravel road. Christy knew they must be nearing their destination, but the journey continued into the night.

"Our only chance is to escape, Victoree," Christy whispered, as she threw her arms around her horse's neck, pressing her face against the long flaxen mane.

Victoree seemed to understand as she nuzzled

the young rider. Christy pushed the horse's head back as she bridled and then saddled the mare. She ran her hands across the straw and hay until she found all of her things. In the darkness, she rolled the pieces into her slicker and tied it back onto the saddle. The grain was gone, but a few things were left from the purchases that she had made at the store.

The first golden streaks of dawn were visible as the truck ground to a halt. Christy knew Bill would not be able to see into the darkness of the truck. As she heard the cab door open, she pulled herself up into the saddle.

"Be ready, Victoree. It's all up to you, girl. You have to save us. Oh, don't get hurt," Christy whispered, as she heard the back door open.

Bill yelled, "Bring the horse here."

Christy squeezed her legs against the horse's sides and shouted, "Now, Victoree, now!"

The horse bolted from the truck. Bill reached for the reins. Christy yanked them away as Victoree's shoulder knocked the dark-haired man to the ground.

"Catch her, Sally," he hollered. "Catch her! Get her, Duke, get her."

The dog tore after the horse and rider, but he was no match for the fleet-footed horse.

"They're heading for the mountains! There's no roads! How can we catch them?" Christy heard Sally scream.

J. FLAGG

Small streaks of orange, yellow, and gold showed in the eastern sky as the girl and her horse raced toward the western darkness.

15

Christy pushed Victoree into a hard gallop. She knew they must make it across the long valley that was barely visible in the faint light of daybreak.

She could hear the slamming of truck doors, the roar of the motor and shifting gears as the kidnappers turned the truck around and raced after her.

"Come on, Victoree! Go, girl!" Christy cried. "We've got to escape. Run!"

The mare laid her neck low and stretched her stride to the limit as she galloped like a runaway horse. Intense fear gripped the young girl as the sound of the truck came closer. Suddenly it was beside them. Victoree veered to the left. The cruel driver swung the truck to follow, this time trying to hit the fleeing horse. Again, Victoree changed directions. Just in time, Christy could make out the markings of an old rutted road.

"Watch it, Victoree. Jump!" she yelled, as she cued the mare.

Victoree lunged across the narrow road just before the truck hit a deep furrow and spun out of control. One wheel broke off, flew through the air, and narrowly missed the racing horse and rider. Christy glanced over her shoulder just in time to see the truck tip onto its side. She could hear angry voices shouting at each other. Soon all was quiet as the distance widened between her and the fraudulent couple.

At last, Christy slowed the sweating mare down to a trot. As the sun broke over the horizon, the tired horse and trembling girl entered a pine tree forest. Branches slapped against the horse's sides and the rider's face and body.

"You were wonderful, Victoree. I can't believe we got away. I'm so scared," Christy said, through quivering lips. "What are we going to do now? Walk, girl. You need to cool down. Ouch, that branch hurt. Easy, take it easy, pretty girl."

A thin line of blood trickled down Christy's cheek. Again a branch hit her as they pushed their way through the trees. Christy dismounted, loosened the saddle, and led her horse. The forest floor was covered with brown pine needles, old branches, fallen trees, and short new seedlings.

Christy's legs ached as she picked a pathway that was large enough for the Arabian mare to follow. Several times she had to break branches or turn back and take another route.

"Victoree, do you hear that?" Christy cried. "It sounds like rushing water. Come on this way. We can make it."

The pair struggled through more brush and fallen trees. The silence of the foothills was only broken by the sound of breaking branches, the swiftly moving water, and a raven crowing in the distance.

"Oh, look, Victoree!" Christy exclaimed. "There it is."

The foaming mountain stream tumbled over shining rocks and shimmering stones. Here and there small, jagged boulders broke through the surface, causing small rapids to appear.

Both the Arabian mare and the young girl thirstily drank their fill of the sparkling clear water. Once again the canteen was filled.

Christy sat down on a nearby large rock and for the first time looked at her surroundings. The only narrow clearing was along the stream. Downstream would lead them back towards the kidnappers. The only thing to do was follow the small river higher into the rugged foothills.

"I'm sure those mean people can't find us now, Victoree. Their truck is broke, and they can't catch us on foot. We've got to keep going though," Christy said, once again patting the horse's neck. "We can't stay here. We've got to find some way out and somewhere to hide. That mean man will find some way to try and follow us. I'm so sorry I got us into this. I don't know what to do."

Tears started to cloud Christy's blue eyes and when she could no longer hold them back, she laid her face against Victoree's mane and sobbed uncontrollably. The gentle mare stood quietly as if she understood the need for Christy to cry.

At last Christy brushed the tears away, leaned over the mountain stream and washed her burning face and swollen eyes.

"Let's go, Victoree," Christy said. "We've got to keep moving."

The narrow clearing beside the mountain stream often was not wide enough for Christy and Victoree to follow. Several times Christy had to rein her horse into the treacherous water. The slippery, smooth rocks would slide out from under the horse's feet. Once the mare fell to her knees.

"Easy, pretty girl. Be careful. Whoa, Victoree. Now take it slow," the rider coaxed the nervous mare. "That's a girl. We're almost past those big rocks."

A short time later, they emerged from the cold water. The mountain brook made a needle-sharp turn to the left. Christy gasped as they rounded the bend. There was the most spectacular view that she had ever seen. Huge, rugged, snowcapped mountains loomed above the pine trees in the distance. A waterfall cascaded down the mountain side. Little snatches of rainbow colors danced in the churning waters. All the pictures that Christy had ever seen of the Rocky Mountains could not compare to the beauty before her.

"Oh, Victoree, it's so beautiful. I always dreamed of riding in the mountains. I . . . I can't believe we are really here. What a beautiful, beautiful place."

A soft breeze rustled the pines, and momentarily, the teenager forgot her fears and tried to absorb the scene before her. She never wanted to forget this enchanted place.

16

It had been several hours since Christy had left the exquisite mountain scene. Both horse and rider were exhausted from the day's ride. The clear, pine scented air was thin at this high altitude, and Victoree was puffing as they climbed higher and higher.

Finally the dense forest gave way to sparsely growing trees. Then suddenly the trees stopped and Christy rode Victoree into a lush, grass-covered meadow. Ahead lay a beautiful green valley, which held a crystal blue lake on the one side. The snow covered peaks loomed high in the distance.

"Oh, Victoree. We can stop and rest here. Let me take your bridle off so you can eat," Christy said. "Here, stick your nose in this halter. I'll even pull your saddle off for a while. Bet that feels good."

Christy tied the lariat to the halter and around a tree that they had just passed. Victoree dropped her head to graze.

The young girl ate as little as possible of her meager supply of food. She spread her only blanket under the tree, and lay down, and quickly fell into a troubled sleep. She awoke every few minutes to see Victoree still eating the rich green grass. Later, when she woke again, Victoree was lying down not far from her. Christy smiled and laid back into the blanket. Both the horse and the young rider slept.

Christy woke with a start as Victoree leaped to her feet. Just a short ways from them stood a huge moose. The large animal seemed to have no fear of them, as Christy grabbed the lariet and pulled Victoree closer. She had read somewhere that a moose was one of the most dangerous animals to encounter on a trail.

Victoree moved nervously back and forth as Christy saddled and bridled the mare.

"Hold still, girl," Christy whispered. "We'll get away. Steady, Victoree, easy. Let me on."

Christy grabbed her blanket and hurriedly mounted her horse. The bull moose pawed some dirt and shook its head. The young girl knew the angry animal was about to charge. She also knew if they raced away, the moose would follow.

"Back, Victoree, back," Christy whispered. "Keep facing him. Come on, back into the trees."

The tense mare responded to the frightened girl's commands. Slowly, one step at a time, they backed into the pine trees. The moose moved a few steps forward. Suddenly it dropped its head and charged, crashing through the trees at breakneck speed.

Christy had no time to think or rein Victoree to the side. As the moose charged toward Victoree's left shoulder, the mare reared high on her hind legs. She knocked branches against Christy's head and shoulders as she stepped backwards on her hind legs. The moose passed within inches of the horse's stomach.

Christy lay low on the saddle and hung on as Victoree swirled and raced back to the open meadow. Christy never looked back to see if the moose was following. When they came to the lake at the far end of the meadow, Christy slowed Victoree down.

"We're okay, Victoree. You saved us again," Christy said, as she looked over her shoulder. "He's not coming, he turned back."

J. FLAGG

17

Christy rode her horse to the far side of the lake, putting as much space as possible between her and the enraged moose. By the time they reached the other side, the sun had dropped low in the western sky. She was shocked to see her horse's breath as the evening air changed to a cold mountain chill. She breathed deeply and felt the icy sensation of the cold air deep in her lungs. Christy shivered uncontrollably, not only from the cold, but the frightening prospect of spending the night in these beautiful, but deadly, mountains.

There were huge, red rocks that looked as if they had tumbled down the mountainside many years ago. Darkness falls quickly in the Rocky Mountains. When the panic stricken girl could no longer see, she knew they had to stop. She slid from the horse's back and led the nervous mare among the large boulders. Several crimson rocks formed a three sided shelter. At last the young rider pulled the saddle from the horse's back.

"I hate to take your saddle off, Victoree, but I know your back must be tired. If something happens, I'll just have to jump on and ride you bareback. Let me brush you. I wish I had some oats for you, but they're all gone."

A quiver ran up the girl's spine as a wolf howled in the distance. Victoree moved nervously as the eerie sound pierced the stillness surrounding them. The night seemed to last forever, as strange sounds startled the girl and the horse. Here and there an owl screeched, or a branch cracked. The lone wolf howled again and again. Even splashing sounds of the fish, leaping out of the nearby water to catch a bug, were magnified by the quietness of the vast mountain region. A sliver of a yellow moon and faraway twinkling stars cast shadows across the rocks, which seemed to move as the night lingered on.

Christy wrapped the soft blanket over her winter jacket and pulled it tightly around her legs. Still, she was so cold. She leaned against the warm body of the now relaxed mare. Victoree stood quietly. The welcome warmth helped a little as Christy put her cheek against the satin neck.

"We'll freeze up here, Victoree. We've got to find a way out," the girl muttered, through chattering teeth. The large brown eyes of the Arabian mare looked as if she understood.

At last the faint rays of dawn colored the eastern horizon. With fingers that ached from the bitter cold, Christy led the rested horse from the rock shelter. After Victoree had drank from the lake, Christy took her to a grassy area to graze. The young girl constantly searched the mountainside, the trees, rocks, and even the lake for any sign of danger. A mule deer drank water on the far side of the lake. A doe and her two half-grown fawns grazed in the lush green meadow where the horse and rider had slept the day before. All was at peace as the morning sun rose and warmed the cold, rugged Beartooth Mountain Range of southern Montana.

18

Christy had no idea where they were and would not even have known what direction they were going if the morning sunrise and the evening sunset had not pointed the way.

"I don't even know how long we've been gone from home, Victoree," Christy said, as she bridled and saddled the patient mare. "I'm so hungry and I only have a few crackers left. I don't even know what state we are in. We are just lost somewhere in the mountains—and maybe, maybe we'll never find our way out."

Overtaken by sobs of desperation, Christy fell to her knees. Victoree nuzzled the crying girl's shoulder. Christy threw her arms around the beautiful mare's neck as she continued to weep.

"Victoree, we can't die up here in the mountains. We can't let your baby die. We have to keep moving. Somewhere there has to be a road or maybe even a cabin. I know some of Dad's friends stay in a cabin when they go hunting, or maybe that was a lodge. I don't know for sure."

Another day passed slowly as the lonely pair climbed even higher as they searched for a road or path. The mountains had turned to cliffs and stones, with only small patches of grass. Christy could see snowcapped mountains for miles in every direction.

She guided Victoree across the sharp rocks and around the huge boulders that blocked their way. A chill settled in the air as the sun again descended in the western sky.

They came to the mouth of a large cave that was even big enough for Victoree to enter.

"We better stay in this cave for tonight, girl. I wish I had some matches to start a fire. I never thought we would need them. Come on, Victoree. Get in there," Christy said, as the horse veered to the right.

Christy reined the mare back toward the cave. Victoree stopped and whirled to the left. Christy was about to scold the nervous mare when a deep growl came from the depths of the cave. Just as quickly, small rocks started tumbling down the mountainside as an enormous grizzly bear came crashing through the opening and raised himself to his full height. Christy lost her grip on the reins as Victoree leaped the rocks in front of them and at top speed, raced around boulders and across loose stones. Christy could hear the crashing sound as the bear bore down on them. She almost could feel the hot breath of the grizzly's mouth as the running horse lost her footing and the mare and rider plunged over the mountainside. Landing on a grass slope, Victoree got up. She quickly shifted her weight so she could lift one bruised foreleg off the ground. Blood trickled from a gash in her side. The mare stood dazed and confused as she looked toward her young rider lying unconscious nearby. One broken rein dangled from the bridle bit. The horse hobbled closer to the girl. She touched Christy with her soft muzzle, but the rider did not move. Victoree stood faithfully by.

The grizzly bear peered over the edge, lost interest in the two figures far below, and returned to the cave. It would not be long before the huge animal would lie down and hibernate throughout the long winter months soon to come.

19

The morning of the second day after the fall, Christy began to regain consciousness. The copper colored horse perked up her ears and nudged her gently as the girl's eyes fluttered open.

"Where am I? Oh, Victoree, you are here. What happened?"

Slowly the horrible scene of the grizzly came back to her. She looked up to the cliff and shuddered as she thought of the terrible fall both she and Victoree had survived. She noticed Victoree holding one foreleg up and the dried blood on her side.

"Are you okay? Victoree. Let me see your leg." Christy sat up and ran her hands over the canon bone.

"It's not broken, pretty girl. I was so scared you were hurt, but you'll be all right. I'll wrap it and it will feel a lot better. You are such a good horse. You stayed with me, you didn't run away. You are so special," Christy said, as she started to get up. Her legs buckled beneath, her and she fell back to the ground.

Again she started to get up. She was so weak that she just could not stand. Finally, by holding onto the stirrup, she was able to balance herself against the horse. She fumbled with the buckles on the saddle bag and after several minutes managed to get it open. Christy ate all of her remaining crackers and found one hard piece of candy. Feeling extremely weak, she let herself slide back to the ground. As the sun again warmed the mountainsides, something glistened a short distance away. The canteen. Christy crawled to it and thirstily drank the remaining water.

"I'll be better pretty soon, Victoree. Hang on and I'll wrap your leg in a little while. You saved my life again, pretty girl. What a wonderful horse you are."

Later that day, Christy knew she had to find water for Victoree. She took one of her shirts, tore it in strips and, sitting on the ground, she wrapped the mare's leg. Then holding onto the saddle for support, she led Victoree forward. The horse limped along as the two of them set out on their painful journey.

Along the way, Christy saw a bush covered with bright red berries. They stopped and the young girl ate the sour fruit.

"I hope these aren't poison," she said.

A small stream, barely a foot wide, was found in the late afternoon. Victoree quickly stuck her soft muzzle into the refreshing water and drank.

Christy filled the canteen and leaned against a nearby rock.

"We better stay right here, girl. It's getting dark, and I'm so weak." She pulled her one blanket around her.

The night was long and cold.

20

Christy shivered as she awoke and saw the dusting of snow across the landscape. Dark clouds hung over the high mountaintops. She was so cold.

"We've got to keep moving, Victoree. There has to be a road or something. Let's follow this long valley. If only we could find a cabin. There has to be one someplace."

Christy, feeling weak and dizzy, could hardly lift the weight of the saddle onto the horse's back. She leaned against the horse's shoulder as the world seemed to spin out of control.

"I've got to find something more to eat, Victoree. I'm so sick. I'm scared we are never going to get home." Christy sobbed.

The mare nickered softly as if she understood. She moved forward just far enough for the young girl to climb into the saddle.

"I can't ride you when you have a sore leg. Let me hang onto the saddle horn and I'll walk."

Together the two started down the snow-speckled green valley. The cold night air must have helped the swelling and soreness in Victoree's leg. The horse no longer limped.

"Are you okay, pretty girl?" Christy asked as she rubbed her hands over the bruised area. "It must be well. Victoree, I can't walk any farther. Hold still while I get on."

Christy, once mounted, checked the saddle bags one more time. There was nothing left, not even a crumb. She thought about how she had read somewhere that people had eaten insects to stay alive. Her stomach turned; she knew she would get too sick to even try. Maybe they would find another bush filled with berries.

Large flakes of snow started to drift slowly to the ground. The horse and rider moved on, knowing it would not be very long until even a path or road would be snow covered and lost from view.

Late that afternoon, with snowflakes gently falling around them, the pair finally came to an old rutted dirt road. Christy's heart leapt with joy.

"This has to lead someplace, Victoree," she said, as she turned the horse to head down the mountain. She pulled her blanket over her shoulders as she tried to shield her face from the wet snow. When the road crossed a little mountain stream, Christy let the Arabian mare drink, but she did not get out of the saddle. She felt so weak that she was certain she would not have the strength to get back on her horse.

Christy hung onto the saddle horn as they started out again.

As another day was coming to an end, a cold icy wind came out of the north. The once gentle snow fall became a violent storm, blowing snow across the old road and soon piling drifts against the rocks and stones. The once visible road was disappearing from view.

Victoree moved on until she felt the young girl

slip from the saddle and fall to the ground. The horse waited patiently for her rider to get up.

Christy laid so very still as snow swirled around her. Still Victoree waited.

21

The temperature was dropping fast. A high wind had started to blow, and huge flakes of snow were falling faster by the minute. A real mountain blizzard was in the making.

The tense horse nudged the unconscious girl. Christy did not move. Then, hearing a noise coming from the trail they had traveled, Victoree circled the young girl and stood protectively between Christy and the noise as it came closer.

Suddenly figures emerged from the blinding snow.

"What in the world is that?" a snow-covered, heavily bearded man exclaimed.

He pulled his bay mustang to a halt and was about to dismount when Victoree bared her teeth, laid back her ears, and reared up on her hind legs. A large, hairy black dog moved up beside the mustang and was about to bark at the strangely acting horse.

"Back, Buckaroo, back. Stay," the bearded man commanded.

He pulled the mustang back a few steps, then quietly dismounted.

"Crazy horse. What are you doing up here and where did you come from?" Joshua Jacobson asked as he tried to calm the frightened mare. "If I don't get you out of here, you'll starve or freeze to death. You don't look like no mountain horse to me."

Again Victoree reared, pawed the air, and would have struck the man if he had moved closer. It was then that Joshua saw Christy lying on the old road, almost covered with snow. Joshua wanted to grab the mare's rein to pull the horse out of the way, but he knew it was to dangerous. He moved cautiously forward a small step at a time.

Again the mare laid back her ears and reared slightly as if to warn the man not to come any closer.

"I need your help, Buckaroo. Come up here. Sit."

The man and dog moved a few steps closer to Victoree. The horse watched both of them and snorted a warning.

"Down, Buck, down."

The dog crouched low to the ground and inched forward.

"Fetch, Buckaroo, fetch," Joshua said, as the dog came to the bridle rein where it laid in the snow. "Down, boy, down. Fetch."

The dog's belly dropped in the snow as he picked up the rein and brought it back to his master. Joshua stooped low and took hold of the leather. Victoree felt the rein tighten and knew she could not back away. She tried to shy away from the stranger as he continued to talk to her. At last he was able to get the horse to smell his hand. He petted her on her muzzle and then led her forward, away from the motionless girl.

Joshua Jacobson was a good hand with horses. He moved slowly and cautiously as he talked softly to the nervous mare. Victoree kept looking back at Christy as the man tied her to the nearest tree.

Joshua then lifted the unconscious girl onto the bay mustang. He wrapped her in her blanket and laid her across the saddle. He took the lariat and tied the blanket securely around the girl. Then he tied her on the saddle. There had been many times when he had tied an animal this way. The mustang stood quietly.

"Come on, Bay Boy. Come, Buckaroo. We've got to make it to the cabin before we get stranded and this poor girl freezes to death. Looks like quite a storm churning up."

Joshua led the bay horse up beside Victoree. He untied Victoree and, leading the two horses, headed into the raging snowstorm. His high boots were lined and fit tight against his legs. His heavy sheepskin coat hung long over a heavy knit sweater and a warm flannel shirt. He was prepared for winter in these Rocky Mountains.

They trudged on through the swirling snow. Finally Joshua turned into a small clearing. A dark cabin and an old weathered building came into view.

A short time later, the nearly frozen, unconscious girl was laying on an old mattress pulled close to a burning fireplace. Still she did not move.

Joshua warmed some canned soup but he had little success in getting Christy to swallow a few spoonfuls. She was still unconscious, maybe even starving.

The walls of the old cabin creaked as the howling wind piled deep drifts against the mountain home.

J. FLAGG

Even though Joshua had neither radio or television, he knew what this storm would be. High in the mountains, it could be deadly. He was thankful they had made it to the cabin in time. He knew his young patient should be taken to a doctor. That too was an impossibility. Even if he had a telephone, there would be no way anyone could come. He would do the best he could to save her.

Victoree was in the makeshift barn. She was shivering as the wind whistled through the open cracks in the old walls. The hay before her was old and dusty. She nibbled at it a few times. She was cold and tired.

Back in the cabin, Joshua put more logs on the fire, then lay down on the handmade bed in the corner. He blew out the flame in the old metal lantern. There was no more he could do this night.

22

Two days passed as Christy went from unconscious to semiconscious and back again. She never really woke up enough to know where she was or how she got there.

Joshua was able to feed her a small amount of the soup that he had fixed. Her eyes never focused on him nor was she aware of the soup being placed in her mouth.

The mountain man had watered Victoree and put the best hay he had out for her. Victoree's eyes were dull and lifeless. Joshua had blanketed her. Still the mare shivered as the storm raged on.

It was in the early evening of the fourth day when Joshua again lit the old lantern. Dark shadows danced across the cabin walls. His shadow looked gigantic as it flickered back and forth on the stone fireplace.

Christy screamed. The black dog growled a warning.

"Now, now, little girl, everything is okay. Lay down, Buckaroo, you be quiet," Joshua said, as he carried the lantern across the room.

Christy's eyes were wide with terror as the big burly man came closer. She covered her face with the blanket and expected it to be ripped from her body. Instead, the man spoke softly.

"Don't be frightened, little lady. I found you and your horse half frozen on the old road up here. You've been pretty sick. What's your name and how did you get way up here? Oh, by the way, my name is Joshua. You can call me Josh if you'd like."

Christy stayed covered but quickly questioned the large man.

"My horse, where is my horse? I've got to find her! What happened to her?" Christy cried, as she threw the blanket back and tried to jump to her feet. Her weak legs promptly buckled beneath her. She fell back on the mattress and sobbed uncontrollably.

"I've got to find her. I—I have to go," she said, as she crawled off the mattress.

"Hey, take it easy. Your horse is out in the barn. Now you relax and try to get some of your strength back. Then I'll take you to see your mare," Joshua answered, as he lifted her back onto the mattress. "I'm going to heat up some more soup, and you try and eat. That's the only way you'll get better."

Joshua moved back across the room.

Christy was glad there was more distance between them. Again, Joshua spoke.

"You still didn't tell me your name or anything about yourself. You are lucky I came along when I did. There won't be much traveling on that road till spring. I barely saw you in the snow, and what a blizzard we had. Lasted two days, quit, and now its snowing again. Rough winter we're having."

Christy pushed back against the mattress as Joshua came with a steaming bowl of soup. "You don't have to be scared of me, little girl. I'm not going to hurt you. Now, here, try and eat this," he said.

Christy mumbled a thank you and took the soup. It tasted good.

"My name is Kelly Ann Jones," she lied, as she thought of the reward money. "I got lost."

Joshua knew there was a lot more to this story. He dropped the subject. He had plenty of time.

23

Christy glanced out of the small cabin window. It was frosted over, but she could still see the snow coming down. It had been a long night.

After eating the hot soup, she had closed her eyes and pretended that she had fallen asleep. Finally Joshua had put more wood on the fire, blew out the old lantern and gone to bed. Buckaroo jumped onto the faded quilt and lay down beside him. Soon Christy could hear the even tempo of Joshua's snoring. She knew he and his dog were asleep.

She had opened her eyes and watched the flickering fire in the fireplace.

I wonder why he is being so nice to me, she thought. Just like the kidnappers had been at first. *He must not know who I am. There's no TV, radio, or even a newspaper. How could he know? He must want Victoree. We have to escape.*

It was then that Christy had decided to go along with this strange man. She would eat his food and answer his questions. She would make up some kind of story. She had to get him to take her to Victoree. Then she and her horse would get away. Finally she had fallen asleep.

Christy had awoke with a start. She couldn't place where she was until she saw Joshua pouring a cup of strong smelling coffee.

Joshua must have been up for quite a while. The fire was burning brightly in the fireplace, and the cabin felt nice and warm.

"Are you awake, Kelly Ann?" Joshua questioned. "I've made some hot cereal. Should help get your strength back. I got sugar but only powdered milk. It's better than nothing."

"Thank you, Mr.—" Christy replied, as she remembered that Kelly Ann Jones was the name she had given him. "I'm not very hungry, but some cereal would be nice."

"Now you just call me Josh. My name is Joshua Jacobson, but Josh is all you need," the man said, as he brought a bowl of steaming cereal.

Christy sat up on the mattress and took the cereal. It was good and she was hungrier than she thought.

"That's the way," Joshua said, as he took the empty bowl. "I can make you some more if you want."

"No, thanks. I'm full," Christy answered. "I can see it is still snowing. Is the barn very far from here? I can hardly wait to see my horse."

"You better take it a little easy. The drifts are six feet deep out there," Joshua said. "The barn isn't very far away, but you are in no shape to plow your way through that much snow. I've already been out and fed your mare and my old mustang. They are getting along just fine. As soon as it quits snowing, I'll shovel a path. Then you can go."

Joshua did not say that Victoree had lost a lot of

weight or that she was not eating well. He felt it would only upset the young girl.

Christy lay back on the old mattress. When would it stop snowing? When would she see Victoree? Would they ever get to go home?

24

"It looks like it will clear up this afternoon," Joshua said. "May not till after dark though."

"How can you tell?" Christy asked. "It's still snowing."

"Look off to the west. See the lighter color? It probably has already quit over there. It's slowing down here too."

Christy got up and went over to the window. She could see the outline of a building a short distance away.

"Is that the barn?" she exclaimed. "I can hardly wait to see Victoree. Can we go out this afternoon?"

"Hold on, Kelly Ann. I have to shovel a path. That snow is pretty deep. I'll get at it as soon as it slows down some more," Joshua replied. "So your mare's name is Victoree. Where did you get her?"

"My dad got her for me. A long time ago," Christy answered, swallowing hard to get the lump out of her throat. She was scared that if Joshua had ever read anything about her, Victoree's name might have been in the article.

Joshua noticed how nervous Christy was. It seemed anytime he asked her a question she was terrified. *What could this young girl possibly be hiding?* Joshua pondered such thoughts and wondered how he could gain the girl's confidence. Maybe taking her to see her horse. He only wished the mare looked better.

"Listen, Kelly Ann. If you want to go see Victoree, I'll carry you. You can hang on my back if you want to. I'm not sure you are strong enough to do that, but we'll try," Joshua said. "We'll take my shovel in case it's too deep and the drifts won't hold us. I could walk on most of them this morning. What do you say?"

Christy flinched as she thought of Joshua touching her. Her love for Victoree was overwhelming. She had to see her horse, she had to agree.

25

The crisp, hard snow crunched beneath Joshua's footsteps as Christy clung to his back. The cold, frosty air looked like silver smoke as Joshua breathed heavily and trudged through the snow. Christy tried to keep her face covered with the old sheepskin jacket that Joshua had given her to wear. Her throat and lungs stung as the cold air entered her body. It seemed so much farther than it looked from the old log cabin.

Suddenly, Christy felt dizzy and weak. Her grip slipped from around Joshua's neck and she plunged into the frozen snow.

"I knew I shouldn't of brought you out here," Joshua uttered, as he lifted Christy into his arms.

"I'm okay. Please don't take me back. Please let me see Victoree. I want to go see her. Please take me," Christy cried out.

"Take it easy, Kelly Ann," Joshua replied. "I'll carry you the rest of the way but we'll only stay a few minutes. You've got to get back where it's warm."

"Thank you, Joshua. Oh, thank you. You are such a nice man," Christy answered.

Joshua felt a surge of joy as he again started the laborious journey to the barn. Maybe at last this young girl was going to trust him. "We are almost there," he said.

Christy had to wait momentarily until her eyes

were able to focus in the sudden darkness of the old barn.

"Victoree, Victoree. Where are you?" she called.

A soft whinny came from the far side of the old building. Christy started to run.

"Hey, take it easy. You're liable to fall again. Here, take hold of my arm and I'll help you," Joshua said as he grabbed her.

Joshua steadied Christy as she stumbled and tried to regain her footing. She felt a sick feeling as she saw the little snowdrifts that had seeped through the cracks in the walls. The air seemed as cold as it had outside.

Victoree was standing next to Bay Boy, the old mustang. Christy's heart sank as she saw the line of the mare's ribs showing through the rough hair of the horse's once beautiful coat. Christy saw the runny nose and the dullness of those once brilliant eyes. She started to cry.

"I've been trying to get her to feel better before I brought you out here, Kelly Ann," Joshua said. "She just doesn't want to eat. Maybe we can make a warm mash out of some of the cereal I got at the house. Come on, Kelly Ann. You've got to get in where it is warm. You are too weak to get so cold."

Christy buried her face against the softness of Victoree's mane and put her arms around the mare's neck.

"I'll be back as soon as I can, Victoree. Please eat and get well. You've got to, pretty girl. You've just got to."

Joshua gently pulled Christy back from the horse. Victoree stepped forward as if to say she didn't want Christy to leave. Tears flowed down Christy's checks as she again hugged the mare's neck.

"We've got to go, Kelly Ann," Joshua urged.

Christy turned to look back one last time before they left the barn. She heard a soft whinny as the door closed behind them.

26

The sky was a vivid blue, and the sun cast colorful rays of light into the rustic cabin. Drops of water dripped from the long icicles that hung along the roof edges. A warm Chinook wind blew across the mountain peaks and meadows. The first winter storm was over.

Christy awoke to the sound of shoveling. She got up and could see Joshua clearing a path to the barn. Maybe Victoree was better. She hurriedly dressed, grabbed the old sheepskin jacket, and rushed out the door.

"Just a minute, Kelly Ann," Joshua called. "You go back in the house and eat some breakfast. You've got to take care of yourself. There's a pot of hot cereal on the back of the stove. I'll have this cleared off by the time you are done."

Reluctantly, Christy went back inside. The cereal did taste good.

Joshua came to the door just as she had finished eating.

"Let's try some more of the mash," he said. "Maybe since your horse is warmer, we can get her to eat this time. There's a small clearing behind the barn without much snow. We'll take the horse out there when the sun gets up over the trees. Old Bay Boy knows how to paw for that green grass. Let's hope Victoree will too."

"I'll dig it out and feed it to her," Christy answered. "She'll eat it then."

"Spoiled horse," Joshua said, with a smile. "She must of lived a pampered life."

Christy shot him a distrustful look. Was he trying to get information about them? She saw the smile and the teasing look in his eyes. She relaxed and knew he was trying to make it easier for her.

"I guess I am guilty of spoiling her a bit," Christy replied, as they headed for the barn.

Victoree would not eat the mash. Christy coaxed and coaxed. Still the mare did not respond. Christy went outside and dug through the snow. She brought a handful of grass back to the sick horse. Victoree nibbled a little, then turned her head.

"Just wait, Kelly Ann," Joshua said. He tried to keep the apprehension from his voice. "It will be warmer outside before long. We'll take her outside then. Maybe that will help."

Joshua knew he had to do something and do it right away. The mare was getting worse.

Both horses seemed to enjoy getting out in the sunshine. Bay Boy immediately pawed through the snow to the lush grass below. Victoree would take a few bites from Christy's outstretched hand, and then she refused to take anymore.

Joshua watched as the worried girl begged the mare to eat. He knew there was only one thing left to do. Try to get that horse down the mountain.

27

It was late that same evening. The horses were back in the barn. Christy was toying with the food on her plate. Joshua spoke up. "Kelly Ann, you have to eat and keep your strength up. We have a long hard trip in front of us. We will take Victoree down the mountain to Johnny Parnell's place. They've got some mighty good horses there, and Johnny knows how to take care of them. It's the only thing I can think of to do."

"Thank you, Joshua, for trying so hard to make Victoree well. She saved my life at least three times. I can't bear to loose her. She's all I have," Christy said, as she tried to hold back the overflowing tears. "Joshua, my name is Christy. I'm sorry I lied to you."

"Don't you worry about that now, young lady. We've got some packing to do. We'll put your saddle on Bay Boy, and you can ride him. We'll need to take all of our blankets and some food and water. Depending on the trail, it may take us a couple of days. You know, Christy is a pretty name. I like it better than Kelly Ann. Come on, let's get everything ready. We'll have to leave at daybreak."

The sun was just peeking over the horizon when Joshua shook Christy and told her breakfast was ready.

"Better eat plenty," he said. "It's going to be a long hard trip."

Christy was full of questions, but there wasn't time to ask them now. Maybe Johnny Parnell would know who she was. It was just a chance that she would have to take. She knew Victoree needed help. That was all that mattered.

Soon the little caravan was on its way. Joshua was in the lead. He carried his shovel and used it several times to clear the trail of rocks or when the snow was to deep. Buckaroo bounced over broken branches and lunged through the deeper snow off the main trail. He found a rabbit to chase that quickly scurried away.

Christy sat in her saddle, barely visible between blankets, bedrolls, saddle bags full of food, and even a bundle of wood tied securely behind the saddle. The old mustang was as surefooted as a mountain goat. He carefully picked his way along the obscure trail. Victoree followed behind. Christy's lariat was tied to her halter and then to the saddle on Bay Boy.

"How are you doing, Christy? Are you all right?" Joshua asked.

"I'm okay," she answered, even though she felt cold and awfully tired.

"We'll stop every so often and give Victoree a rest. You better get down when we do. Move around a bit. You'll feel better if you do."

"Okay, I will. How far is it?" Christy questioned.

"About twenty to twenty-five miles. Something like that. We'll have to camp out tonight."

The day was long and treacherous. Victoree had stumbled and fallen onto her knees. Christy wanted to stop.

"We have to keep moving, Christy. These mountains can be deadly if another storm blows on. I know it's hard to force Victoree, but we have to. It's the only way we can save her. We'll rest a few minutes and then move on," Joshua said as he checked Victoree's legs for any bruises. He was beginning to wonder if the Arabian mare would make it. He had to try.

28

Nightfall comes quickly in the Rocky Mountains. When the sun drops behind the mountain peaks, darkness is only minutes away.

Christy stroked Victoree's neck and tried to get her to eat.

"Why don't you tie a couple of blankets over her, Christy? It'll keep the chill off and make her feel better. We got plenty and we have the bedrolls," Joshua called, as he lit the campfire.

It wasn't long before Victoree lay down. Christy pulled the blankets over her and held the mare's head on her lap.

"You've got to hang on, pretty girl. We'll get there tomorrow. Joshua says this man can help you. Please, Victoree, please don't die." Christy whimpered.

"There, there, little girl. Let her rest. You come and eat your supper. Then you get some sleep. I'll watch over Victoree tonight," Joshua said, as he helped Christy to her feet.

"I don't think I can sleep. I'm so worried, I just wish it wasn't so far."

"We did just fine today. We are over halfway, and the trail gets a lot better now. It cuts into a road a short way from here. Then we can follow the road to Parnell's."

Christy slept off and on through the night. Coyotes yelped in the distance. A full moon rose in the clear dark sky. Christy could see Joshua checking Victoree, dragging some old log pieces, brushing them off, and putting then on the smoldering campfire. Sparks danced above the flames as the wetness of the wood sizzled on the fire. Then all was quiet. Christy, completely exhausted, fell back asleep.

Again, Joshua shook Christy and woke her for breakfast. Before she would eat, she rushed to Victoree's side. The mare was standing. She perked up her ears a little and laid her head on Christy's shoulder. "It will be a better day today, pretty girl. We'll soon be on a road. You'll be better soon," Christy said, as she brushed the forelock from the horse's eyes.

"Come on, Christy. We better get going. You eat and I'll break camp," Joshua called, as he saddled Bay Boy.

Again, the caravan started down the trail. Two hours had passed by the time they reached the old mountain road.

"I thought it would be a gravel road," Christy said, showing her disappointment. "Not just a couple of rutty tracks."

"You are in the mountains, little girl. This is a road. It is mostly used by four-wheelers. Snowmobilers like to come up here in the winter too."

Christy nodded her head in agreement. Her shoulders ached, her legs hurt. She was too tired to really care.

Suddenly Victoree fell. Joshua ran back to the

horse as Christy jumped from the saddle. The weak mare would not get up. She lay flat on her side. She sighed softly and closed her eyes. She no longer would raise her head even when Christy coaxed her. The ailing horse was ready to give up.

Christy burst out crying as she pulled the horse's head toward her.

"Leave her be, Christy. Just stay with her. Here, cover her with these blankets. I'll go for help," Joshua said, as he threw all but the saddle from Bay Boy's back. "Buckaroo, you stay."

With that Joshua was gone.

29

Christy had heard the sound of the galloping horse fade into the distance. She felt so alone. Finally she crawled under the blankets with Victoree and waited. The horse never moved. Buckaroo lay nearby.

Victoree's breathing was shallow and raspy. Tears streamed down the girl's face which she hardly noticed. The minutes seemed like hours. What could Mr. Parnell do for Victoree lying way out here? Again guilt overwhelmed the girl.

"If only I had gone to that stupid girl's school, you would be all right, Victoree. I feel so bad. I wish Dad was here. He would know what to do," Christy sobbed, wiping the tears from her eyes.

Buckaroo lifted his head as she spoke. Then, abruptly, the dog got to his feet, the hair stood up on his back and a low growl came from deep within the animal's throat.

Christy shook with fear as Buckaroo came toward her. Then she noticed the dog's eyes were focused on the trees behind them. Buckaroo slowly circled the girl and her horse until he was directly between them and the nearby trees.

A piercing scream shattered the mountain air. A bolt of fear raced through Christy as she saw a large, crouched mountain lion leap from a nearby tree. Buckaroo was ready and hurled himself toward the animal's throat. The snarling cougar swung loose and grabbed the dog by his neck. A yelp of pain came from Buckaroo. Flesh tore as the dog tried to free himself.

Christy turned away. She couldn't watch. Again there was a cry of pain. Then a shot rang out. The mountain lion dropped to the ground. Buckaroo, limping and bleeding, pulled himself free.

A tall, young man, carrying a long-barreled shotgun, walked over to the mountain lion and pushed the animal with his boot. The lion lay still.

Running past him to the wounded dog was Joshua.

"I knew you'd take care of them, boy. Here, let me see your leg. That neck wound is a nasty one, but it's not deep. Stay, I'll get some bandages," Joshua said. "The horse is under those blankets. Go ahead with the mare. I'll take care of my dog."

"Hi, Christy. I'm Johnny Parnell. Joshua told me your name. Let's see your horse."

Victoree's eyes opened as she felt the touch of the stranger. Still, she did not try to get up.

"I guess we better get some IV fluids into her, and I'll give her a shot of Banamine. That'll get her back on her feet," Johnny said. "We'll get her in the horse trailer and take her down to the ranch."

"Mr. Parnell, will—will she be all right?" Christy asked.

"I think she's got maybe a 50-50 chance. I won't promise, but I think so. It will take some time though."

Johnny had said horse trailer. Christy turned and saw the silver colored, four-wheel drive pickup with the matching trailer.

"It will take about twenty minutes for the shot to take hold," Johnny said, as he picked up the case of medicine. "I better check on Joshua's dog. He may need a few stitches and a bandage or two. I guess we got back here just in time. You hold this IV bottle about this high. Keep it at this level. I'll be right back."

30

The two men had to lift and push Victoree to finally get her up. She stood with her front legs far apart to balance herself. Christy petted her forehead and talked softly to her.

"Let her stand a minute. Christy, you stay at her head and keep talking to her. Maybe you can kind of balance her, Joshua, if she gets wobbling too much. I'll back the trailer up as close as I can."

Christy guided the horse while the two men lifted first one front leg and then the other into the enclosed trailer. Victoree stepped forward. At last Victoree was loaded. She leaned slightly against the side but stayed standing.

"I'll ride back here with her, if that's okay," Christy said.

"Good idea. The road's kind of rough. If you need us, shove one of those little feed doors open. We'll watch for it."

Joshua carried Buckaroo and laid him on the pickup floor. The dog whined a bit when he was moved. Johnny Parnell had said he would be sore for a few days but would be all right. Christy was relieved and happy for Joshua.

It was a rough ride, even in the slick new pickup. The trailer was worse. Victoree still managed to stand.

Long shadows lay across the road. It was late afternoon when Johnny turned under a large ranch sign. Christy could read the big bold letters—Mystic Mountain Ranch. *What a beautiful name,* she thought.

The snow had been plowed. A smooth gravel driveway circled the large open space in front of the buildings. Johnny stopped the pickup in front of a massive log barn. The long sloping roof was a deep green, almost the color of freshly mowed grass. The barn had been stained a rich rustic color. Everything was neat and clean. It was picture perfect, with the towering snow-covered mountains in the background.

The medication that Johnny had given Victoree had taken hold. The mare backed out of the trailer and was able to walk slowly into the barn. A large, thickly bedded box stall was opened for her. Johnny put up some heat lamps overhead to warm the stall. Victoree lay down in the fresh straw.

"She's had a rough trip. Better let her rest. We'll check on her a little later," Johnny said. "Come on up to the house. You both look like you could stand a hot meal."

"I would rather stay with Victoree," Christy answered. "Maybe she would feel better if she knew I was here."

"Okay, Christy. I understand. I'll bring you something to eat when I come back to check on Victoree," Johnny replied. "Joshua, come on up to the house and bring Buckaroo in. He needs a nice warm place to lay down too."

31

Christy spent two nights in the stall with Victoree. She could hear the sounds of more horses in the line of box stalls, but she hadn't gone to look at them. She couldn't bear to leave Victoree.

It was the third morning when Christy awoke that the mare was up and eating a few bites of hay. Christy was overjoyed. She crawled out of the warm sleeping bag that Johnny Parnell had given her and threw her arms around the horse's neck.

"You're going to be all right, pretty girl. You are going to get well," Christy said, overflowing with joy. "I was so worried and scared. I don't know what I would do without you."

A little later, Joshua and Johnny came into the barn, carrying Christy's breakfast.

"Victoree ate a little hay and some of the grain is gone. Isn't it wonderful?" Christy asked.

"It's a good sign. We still better give her some more IV fluids. We'll give her a shot of Vitamin B-12. Maybe that will build up her appetite. But you, young lady, better come up to the house. I dug through my daughter's closet and found some clothes. I think they'll fit. If we don't get you cleaned up. Victoree won't even want you in her stall," Johnny said, with a smile.

It was midmorning before Christy finished

washing and drying her hair. The shower had felt so good and even thought the shirt and blue jeans were a little big, they felt wonderful.

Christy couldn't believe the size of the log house. It had a massive living room that appeared more like a hotel lounge than a family home. There were several leather chairs, couches, end tables, and a huge fireplace across one end.

Johnny Parnell and Joshua Jacobson were talking as she came down the open wooden staircase. They greeted her and told her to join them. Joshua was the first to speak.

"Buckaroo is feeling pretty good. We're about to head home before the weather acts up again. We'll miss your company, Christy. Johnny and I talked it over, and it's better for you to stay here awhile."

Christy didn't know what to say. She hadn't thought past Victoree getting well, but just to stay here—she didn't know. That old cold barn was no place for her horse either. Johnny spoke up.

"You are welcome to stay, Christy. We'll get that mare of yours back on her feet. The first weekend the roads are opened my family will be up from Billings. The kids go to school down there in the winter. They come up here every weekend they can. They much prefer ranch life to city dwelling."

It wasn't long before Joshua sat on Bay Boy, bareback. Buckaroo was anxious to go.

"It's been nice knowing you, Christy. I still don't know much about you, but I wish you the best," Joshua said. "And thanks, Johnny, for the hospitality and helping me out. And most of all, for saving Buckaroo."

"Think nothing of it. Come back anytime. The coffee pot is always on," Johnny replied.

"Thank you, Joshua. Oh, thank you so much for saving Victoree and me. I'll remember you the rest of my life," Christy said, with a lump in her throat. She hated to see Joshua go.

"I left your saddle in the barn, Christy. Who knows, little girl, our paths may cross again. I hope so," Joshua said. "Take care of that pretty mare."

With a wave of his hand, Joshua rode under the big ranch sign and was soon out of sight.

32

Christy felt a bit uneasy when Joshua left. She had grown to trust the bearded man. He had never questioned her, as he could see that it bothered her. He never even demanded to know her last name. She knew Johnny Parnell would be different. Even now he seemed to be searching her expressions for some answers.

"I think I'll go and see how Victoree is doing. If that is okay with you, Mr. Parnell?" Christy asked.

"Of course, it's okay, Christy. And you can call me Johnny. Everybody else does. Don't worry about being here alone with me. A couple of the winter ranch hands should be here by noon tomorrow. One if them is married to a nice lady who cooks for us. She'll be along too. Her name is Ella. You'll like her," Johnny replied. "They would have gotten here a couple of days ago if we hadn't had the storm. The phone lines are still down, but shouldn't be for long. Then you can call your family and let them know you are okay."

Johnny saw the look of suspicion cross Christy's face. Why did he have this hunch that he should know something about this girl? *What was she hiding? Where had she come from?* These were some of the questions that Johnny wanted to know the answers to. Joshua didn't seem to know anything either. About the only think he had said was Christy had told him her name was Kelly Ann Jones, but she later had said her real name was Christy. That was all.

Johnny watched as Christy made her way to the barn. Then he turned and went back to the house.

"I sure wish Marlene and the kids were here. They might be able to get some answers from her," Johnny muttered to himself as he hung up his jacket. Just as he was pouring another cup of coffee, the telephone rang. After a short conversation with the company about the lines being repaired, Johnny called his wife.

"Hello," Marlene answered.

"Hi, Hon. They finally got this phone working," Johnny said. "I sure have missed talking to you. Are you and the kids all right?"

"We're fine, Johnny. They got the streets plowed here the day after the storm. Mickey's school was closed for the day, but the twins didn't miss any. How about you?"

"Everything's okay. Sid, Ella, and Jimmy got held up. They should be back today."

"And you have to do all the feeding by yourself," Marlene said with a chuckle. "I'll bet you weren't too happy about that."

"Not exactly. Joshua Jacobson was here and helped. A few days ago he came tearing up the drive full blast wanting me to help him. This mare was down on the old road, not too far from his cabin. Had this young girl that he found half froze on the trail north of his place. Guess they had been at his cabin a week or more. You know Josh, doesn't say much."

"What did you do? Are they all right?" Marlene asked.

"The mare, looks like an Arabian, is back on her feet but still pretty poor. The girl is as skinny as a rail, but seems to be okay. She's out in the barn now. Funny thing is, Joshua had no idea who she is or how she got up on that old trail. All we know is her name is Christy. Anyway, that's what she says. Seems to be hiding something."

"That's odd. How old is she?" Marlene asked.

"I'd say about the age of Michael and Michelle. Maybe a little younger. I don't know. It's a good thing I got to that horse when I did. She wouldn't have lasted long," Johnny replied. "Wish you were here. You'd do a lot better at getting that girl to talk."

"If the roads aren't too icy, I'll be up this weekend. The kids will really want to come now. It's quite a mystery," Marlene responded. "Johnny why don't you check 'Missing Persons' on the Internet? There might be something there."

"That's a good idea. I'll do it right away."

33

"Johnny! Mr. Parnell! Come quick. Victoree laid down and I can't get her up," Christy screamed, as she raced for the house.

Johnny flicked off the computer and hurried to the door.

"What's wrong?" he called, as the panic-stricken girl ran toward him.

"It's Victoree. She's down and in a lot of pain. She's breathing real hard. I think she's dying," Christy sobbed.

Johnny grabbed his jacket and rushed past the girl to the barn. His long legs ate up the distance in seconds. She was lying on the stall floor. Her sides heaved in and out.

Christy rushed into the stall.

"Is she dying? What's wrong with her? She seemed all right this morning," the young girl cried.

Johnny felt the horse's pulse. It was throbbing, but it was rhythmic in its beat. The mare's sides heaved again, and her legs stiffened as she strained inside of herself.

Johnny knew what was wrong.

"Do you know when Victoree is due to foal?" Johnny asked.

"Not until after Christmas," Christy answered. "Is she having her colt?"

"I believe so. And Christmas is a ways off. I'm

not sure if we can save the foal, even if it is born alive. We'll concentrate on Victoree and do what we can for the colt," Johnny answered, as he listened to the heartbeat again. "So far, so good. Christy, you run down to the tack room and get some of those clean horse blankets. Three or four will do. Better get a pail of hot water too. There's a stainless steel bucket on the shelf. Rinse it out good. Bring that pile of white rags."

It seemed to Christy as if hours had gone by. She sat on the straw-covered floor and held Victoree's head in her lap. The mare was exhausted.

"Come on, don't give up now," Johnny said, as he briskly rubbed the mare's legs and slapped her on the neck. Christy, you better get another bucket of hot water, this one is cold."

Tears streamed down Christy's face, and she took the bucket and left. Quickly, Johnny pulled on the two little forelegs that had come into view. The mare strained with pain as Johnny pulled. The tiny filly was lying on the clean blanket when Christy returned. Johnny dampened a clean rag and cleaned the filly's nose. The foal breathed. She was alive!

34

"She's so tiny," Christy said, as she helped dry the chestnut foal. "All of our foals at home have been twice her size. Is Victoree going to be all right?"

Christy crawled back to the mare. Victoree still lay quietly. She had not even lifted her head to see the little filly. Christy gently stroked the mare's neck. It was still hot and wet with sweat.

"You poor thing. You've got to get well. I'm so sorry, Victoree. I don't know why I ever got you into this. Please get well."

Again the young girl's shoulders shook as she tried to control the pent up emotions that burst forth in sobs.

Johnny pulled the crying girl back from the weakened horse.

"Just let her rest, Christy," Johnny said. "We better get some milk down your filly. I've got some frozen from another mare. You keep rubbing her dry and try to keep her alert. I'll be right back with a bottle."

Johnny hurried out of the stall. He kept thinking about Christy's statement of other foals. She had to be from a horse ranch or stable. It would have to be a place where they raised Arabians. That filly was definitely full Arabian and so was the mare.

If only I had time to check the Internet, Johnny thought. But there was no need to think about that now. It would be touch and go with the filly, and the mare wasn't much better off.

Johnny went back to the stall and lifted the filly to her feet.

"You balance her over my knee. I'll try and get her to take some of this," Johnny said.

"That stuff looks awful. Are you sure it's any good? It's so yellow," Christy replied. "It looks terrible."

Johnny smiled as he saw the look of apprehension cross the teenager's face.

"Don't worry. I wouldn't give your baby anything that wasn't good. The reason it's so yellow is it's rich in proteins and has protective antibiotics in it. It isn't just milk. It is from one of our mares right after she foaled. I always keep some frozen. A foal has to have it to live." Johnny answered. "As soon as Victoree's up and the filly can stand on her own, we'll get your mare to accept her baby."

"How long will that be?" Christy asked.

"I can't answer that. We'll just have to wait and see," Johnny answered. "Hey, she's a feisty little thing. She thinks this stuff is pretty good."

Christy smiled for the first time as she watched the tiny foal's little tail swish back and forth as some of the milk dripped from the teeny muzzle.

"She's so pretty, and she's marked just like her mother. It's a miracle she's alive," Christy remarked.

"Yes, it is. She's a fighter. If we get her through the first twenty-four hours she should make it. Just don't get your hopes up too high," Johnny cautioned. "I'll stay with her all night."

"She'll make it. I know she will. I'm going to name her Mystic Miracle. She is a miracle, and she was born on Mystic Mountain Ranch."

"I like that," Johnny said.

Victoree lifted her head and whinnied softly.

"Victoree likes it too," Christy replied.

35

It had been another long night. The two ranch hands and Ella had arrived around six o'clock. The two men fed the livestock, and Ella cooked dinner while Johnny and Christy stayed with Victoree and her foal. Johnny had tried to persuade Christy to go to the house and eat. Christy had refused. It wasn't long until the ranch hands, Sid and Cody, brought the dinner to the barn. Soon Ella came with some bread pudding. When Johnny had introduced them to Christy, all three got the distinct impression they were not to ask any questions.

A warm sleeping bag was brought in for Christy. Johnny wouldn't let her sleep in the stall, so she had laid as close to the door as possible. Finally, she had fallen into a deep sleep. Johnny remained awake inside the box stall with the two horses.

Christy awoke with a start. She was surprised to see the morning sun streaming in the window. She opened the stall door and saw Victoree, standing with her foal lying at her front feet.

"She's quite the mother," Johnny said. "Your little miracle can't stand by herself yet, but she's doing okay. Why don't you run up to the house and have some breakfast? Ella washed your clothes and you can take a shower. It will do you good. I'll stay here till you get back. Then I'll go in and eat. No need to hurry."

Christy put her arms around the mare's neck and pushed her face against the silky mane. This time she had knew she better do as Johnny asked. She reached down and stroked the filly's soft neck.

"You two be good till I get back. And thank you, Johnny, for everything. I don't know how I'll ever repay you," Christy said.

"There's nothing to repay, Christy. I'm just glad I was at the right place at the right time."

"Were you ever a veterinarian?" Christy questioned.

"Still am." Johnny answered. "Now run along before Ella clears up breakfast."

No wonder he knew what to do and had all that medicine. Christy glanced at the ranch sign. Mystic Mountain Ranch—Johnny and Marlene Parnell—Owners. *He must do most of his practicing medicine on his own stuff,* Christy thought, as she watched a bunch of yearlings play in a nearby pasture.

Breakfast was good, but Ella did fix much more than she could eat. The hot shower felt even better, and it was great to get back into her own clothes.

"I'll run back to the barn so Mr. Parnell can come up for breakfast," Christy called, as she hurried out the door. She could feel Ella's questioning look as she left.

What am I going to tell all these people? What am I going to say, she wondered as she ran across the yard. And in a couple of days, Johnny's family will be coming. What then?

36

"The best thing to do is just leave them alone for a while. Sit here in the corner and watch," Johnny said. "Victoree is tired and still weak. Mystic Miracle, as you call her, has had plenty of milk for now. Come and get me if you need to, but I'm sure everything will be fine. Those bacon and eggs are calling me. Then a shower and I'll be back to check on you. Let them rest, it's the best thing for both of them."

Christy nodded in agreement and settled back in the corner.

"I know you are wondering about the girl. I can't tell you much. All I know is Joshua Jacobson found her half froze on the Old North Trail. She clams up when you ask her anything," Johnny said, as he ate his breakfast. "Tell Sid and Cody not to ask her any questions. I'm going to do my best to find out who she is."

"Okay," Ella replied. "She seems like a nice girl. I wonder where her family is."

"So do I," Johnny said, as he slid away from the table. "So do I."

With that he headed for the shower. A short time later, he went into his office and turned on his computer. He pulled up the Missing Children list and was astounded to find so many names.

"Come on, come on," he breathed, as name after name rolled across the computer screen.

Christina Baldwin, fourteen years old, slight build. Last seen September 4, 1997, riding Arabian horse south of Rochester, Minnesota.

"Could that possibly be her?" Johnny questioned, under his breath as his fingers quickly hit the keys to pull up the girl's web page.

There appearing on the screen was a color picture of Christy on Victoree. There no longer would be questions as to who she was.

Johnny read the rest of the information. "Contact parents: Dr. and Mrs. Walter Baldwin, 1806 Melody Lane, Rochester, Minnesota 55905." He glanced at the telephone number, fax number and e-mail address. Reward $50,000. Or contact the Bureau of Missing Persons.

Johnny printed a copy, turned off the computer, and left the house.

"I can't tell her I know who she is," Johnny muttered to himself. "Maybe she has been abused or something. Who knows? I better check things out before confronting her. A doctor's daughter, and I thought she grew up on a ranch."

"How're our patients doing?" Johnny asked, as he entered the stall.

"They have been resting the whole time you were gone," Christy answered.

"I guess we'd better feed that baby again."

Victoree nickered as they lifted the little filly to

her side. After a few side steps and some nosing around by the foal, breakfast was found.

"It looks like Victoree has plenty of milk. We'll have to help this little gal and make sure she gets plenty to eat," Johnny said. "She's a spunky little thing. Look at her swish that tail and bunt her mother."

Christy's eyes glowed with pride as she helped balance Mystic Miracle.

"I think she'll be the copper color of her mother when she sheds her baby fuzz, don't you?"

"Probably will," Johnny answered. "What color is her sire?"

"Black," Christy answered.

Again Johnny saw the suspicious look that always appeared when he asked Christy a question.

"I'd guess she would stay chestnut. You never know for sure. Some people think a black and chestnut cross is the best way to get a black. I think black colts are usually born black or a gray color. She'll be a beauty, whatever color she is."

Johnny could see Christy's expression relax as he talked.

"I wonder if I should call her Misty for short—or maybe Miracle. No, I think Mystic. That's it, let's call her Mystic."

"Sounds good to me," Johnny replied. "Hang in there, Mystic. You've got a lot of growing to do."

37

Christy sat in the fresh bedding next to Victoree. The mare was lying down and Mystic was stretched out, flat on her side, nearby.

"I don't know what to do now, pretty girl," Christy said, as she petted the horse's forehead. "I would call Mom and Dad, but I'm sure they would come and get me right away. Victoree, you've saved my life over and over again. Mystic is too little to travel, and you aren't very strong either. Dad would want to leave you two here probably until spring. I couldn't stand to be away from you. I want to take care of Mystic and you too."

Victoree pushed her muzzle against Christy's hand. Christy smiled and stroked the mare's neck.

"I won't leave you. I just can't. But what will I tell Johnny and his family? They are coming this weekend."

Mystic scrambled to her feet and stood awkwardly unbalanced before falling back down. Christy laughed at the filly's perplexed expression.

"Come on, little one," Christy said as she urged the little horse to try again. "You can do it."

Again, Mystic stood as Christy steadied her balance. Victoree quickly got to her feet and nickered to her baby. The filly took a few wobbly steps and soon found the warm nourishing milk.

"That's right, little girl," Christy said, as she

J. FLAGG

helped balance the filly. "You better get to growing in a hurry. I don't want anyone to call you a runt. You are so little you can walk right under your mother. Better eat a lot and grow fast, we're a long way from home."

38

"What do you think I should do?" Johnny asked Marlene. He had called her as soon as he got back to his office.

"Is she there? Can she hear you?" Marlene asked.

"No, she's down at the barn. You can hardly even get her to come up and eat or sleep."

"Johnny, why don't you just let things go along the way they are? The kids and I will be up there day after tomorrow. The weather forecast is good. How are the roads?" Marlene asked.

"I think they are pretty good. Probably some icy spots. I'll take the pickup tomorrow and check it down to the highway. Sid and Cody can load some gravel, and I'll throw it on any bad spots. You be careful though," Johnny answered. "Wish you were already here."

"Of course, I'll be careful. How many times have I driven that road? Don't worry," Marlene said. "Back to this young girl. Have you contacted anyone?"

"No, and I think I will wait until we talk to her together. Maybe she's been mistreated or something. She's such a nice kid. Would hate to see her go back to an abusive home. Sure wonder how she ever got to Montana when she was last seen near Rochester, Minnesota."

"That is quite a mystery, isn't it? I hope we can

get her to tell us what happened. We can't just keep her up there on the ranch."

"I know we can't, hon," Johnny replied. "But let's do all we can for her. We'll have to get some answers. Do the kids know she's up here?"

"No, I thought I better not say anything. I'll tell them on the way up. It would be hard for them to keep it a secret. Tell one friend at school and you know how that would spread."

"Like wildfire, I guess," Johnny said. "I better let you go. See you Saturday morning."

"Bye, Johnny. We miss you. We'll be there as early as possible," Marlene answered.

Johnny hung up the phone. *Better check on the filly,* he thought.

"You're quite a horsewoman, Christy. Ever think of becoming a vet? I could use the help in the summertime," Johnny said, as he watched her steady the foal.

Again Christy saw the investigative look on Johnny's face. Christy knew it went much deeper than the question that he had just asked.

"I guess I never thought that far in the future," Christy answered. "Mystic is such is cute little thing. Do you think she will be okay?"

"Looks like it to me. How could she be anything else with all the tender loving care you are giving her?" Johnny asked.

Christy just smiled. Mystic laid down. Victoree munched on the sweet green hay.

"Ella's about ready to put dinner on the table. Everything looks fine here. Let's go eat," Johnny said. "You need a little meat on your bones too."

They left the barn together. *She certainly knows how to cut a conversation short,* Johnny thought, as they walked toward the house.

"Hey, I think I smell fresh baked pies. Ella makes really good ones. I hope it's cherry," Johnny said.

"Me too. That's my favorite," Christy answered, as she breathed a sigh of relief. Maybe Johnny would drop the questions for tonight. Christy wanted time to think.

39

The sky was a cloudless blue as the sun topped the mountains, a picture perfect day was in the making. Johnny had risen earlier than usual. He had already fed Victoree and made sure that Mystic was okay when Christy came down the stairway.

"Good morning, sleepy head," Johnny said, as he tried to engage in light conversation. "I fed your mare, and that little filly is up and around on her own. How about some breakfast before going to the barn? Do you good."

"Okay. I guess I was really tired. Thanks for taking care of Victoree and Mystic. I'm sorry I overslept," Christy replied.

"You needed a good night's sleep. You've been wearing yourself out. Ella's got breakfast ready for you. Maybe she'll even give you another piece of pie," Johnny teased. "Better get your share before my kids come. It will disappear in a hurry."

"Thanks, but I think I'll pass on the pie. I think I ate too much last night," Christy answered, as she hurried into the kitchen. She did want to get to the barn before Johnny's family arrived.

Christy had eaten as quickly as possible and was brushing Victoree when she heard voices coming into the barn. She dreaded the introductions that were about to be made. The stall door swung open as Johnny stepped inside.

"Christy, this is Mickey. And these are my twin teenagers, Michael and Michelle. And here is my wife, Marlene," Johnny said, taking his wife's arm.

"Hello," Christy said, as she looked at each of them. The blonde woman was much shorter than Christy had imagined. She was a very pretty woman. She smiled sweetly and extended her hand.

"I'm glad to meet you, Christy. Johnny has talked about you and your beautiful horses. My, they are pretty ones," Marlene said.

"Can I pet the colt?" Mickey asked as he pushed his way into the stall.

Victoree immediately laid her ears back and moved to protect Mystic.

"You stay back until she gets to know you, Mick," Johnny said. "She's just protecting her baby. All of you kids, stay out of this stall. That mare's been through a lot. We don't want to upset her."

"It's nice to meet you," Michelle said.

"The same goes for me," Michael said. "Boy, were we surprised to hear you were on the ranch. Mom never told us till we were on our way."

"I guess it would be a surprise," Christy answered. "It's nice to meet all of you."

Christy couldn't help noticing how much Michael looked like his dad. Michael and Michelle did resemble each other, except Michael looked so masculine and had the charming good looks of his father. Michelle also had the dark hair and brown eyes. Little Mickey was the only blonde, blue-eyed one, like his mother.

"You kids go unload the car. And I know Ella saved some pie. I think she even has a chocolate one hid away," Johnny said. "Unload the car first."

"Wait for me!" Mickey hollered, as the twins took off running.

Christy felt a twinge of jealousy as the three ran and laughed together. *It must be wonderful to have brothers and a sister,* she thought.

Christy turned back to Victoree and Mystic. Johnny and Marlene were waiting.

"We want to talk to you, Christy," Marlene said. "Don't worry. We just want to talk."

40

"Let's go over to the lounge area by the tack room," Johnny said, as he walked in that direction. "Come on in and sit down, Christy."

Christy made her way to one of the straight-back chairs. Marlene seated herself directly across from her. Johnny remained standing. He reached for the intercom and called the ranch house.

"Hi, Ella. Keep the kids up there for a while, okay? I'll call you or we'll come up pretty soon."

Marlene was the first to speak. She took Christy's trembling hands in hers and held them gently.

"Christy, we know who you are. Christina Baldwin from Rochester, Minnesota. We have no idea how you made it to Montana from Minnesota. We do want to help you."

Christy's face turned a ghostly white at the mention of her name. Montana—it seemed a world away from her home. She felt like a stranger in a foreign land. She glanced at Johnny and felt he had betrayed her. Tears welled up in her eyes as she tried to speak.

Johnny came over and knelt before her.

"Don't cry, Christy. We haven't let anyone know you are here, and we haven't contacted your parents. Take it easy. We are friends, you and I. Good friends, and I want it to stay that way. Can you tell me what happened to you?"

"I was kidnaped," Christy said, between sobs. "I got on Victoree and when they opened the back of the truck, we jumped and escaped. I was so scared that Victoree would get hurt, but she didn't."

"That must have been terrible. We better call your parents and let them know you are all right," Marlene said. "They must be sick with worry."

"No, no! Please don't," Christy cried. "They would come and get me, and Mystic is too little to travel—and—and Victoree needs more time. Please don't."

Marlene and Johnny glanced at each other. Marlene nodded and Johnny began to speak.

"Christy, we have to know. Were your parents mean to you? Did they beat you or something? You seem so scared," Johnny asked.

"No, nothing like that. Mother wanted to send me to a girl's school in Boston. I ran away. I couldn't leave Victoree and not even be with her when Mystic was born. I'm so sorry. They might take Victoree and Mystic away from me now. Victoree almost died. They can't take her away."

Again, uncontrollable sobs wrenched the girl's thin body. Little by little, Christy told her story—the kidnaping, the moose, the grizzly bear, everything.

"Whew, you could write a book," Johnny said. "Let's talk this over. Why don't I call and speak to your dad? I'll tell him you are okay and not to worry. Would you like me to tell him that you will call in a few days when you feel a little better? In the meantime, we'll take care of Victoree and Mystic the way we have been. I won't tell your parents where you are until it's okay with you. How does that sound?"

Christy wiped her swollen eyes with the tissue that Marlene had given her.

"Dad will offer you this big reward, and he'll try to convince you to tell him," Christy answered.

"Hey, Christy, have you forgotten already? We are friends—good friends. You don't take rewards from friends. You just help them out of their troubles. Isn't that right, Marlene?"

Marlene nodded in agreement.

"I would be worried sick if one of my children disappeared. Just imagine what your mother and father are going through. By now they probably feel they will never see you again. Let's let them know you are alive and well. What joy and relief a short telephone call would give them," Marlene said, as she too wiped tears from her eyes.

"I never really thought about them worrying so much—but can't you understand? They'll take Victoree and Mystic away from me because I ran away," Christy cried. "Tell them I am so sorry, I am, I really am. Just please, please don't tell them I am here."

"I promise I won't tell where you are, and I will tell them you are sorry. Okay? But now, first things first. Let's go check on your horses," Johnny replied.

A tiny whinny was heard as Christy opened the stall door.

"She's just like Victoree!" Christy exclaimed.

"Victoree always talks to me when I come in the barn. Isn't she wonderful?"

"That she is," Johnny said, as he watched the young girl embrace the small filly and then throw her arms around the copper colored mare. "They both are," he added, as he thought of what this girl and horse had been through. There's no way a parent could take them away from her, he was sure of that.

41

"Montana. Can you believe that, Victoree? We are in Montana," Christy said, as she caressed the mare's neck.

Mystic nudged the girl's arm.

"You are so much like your mother, little girl. She always does that too when she wants attention." Christy laughed.

The thought of the phone call that she needed to make quickly wiped the smile from her face.

"I want to call them, pretty girl. But what will I say? How can I explain what we did? What will they do to me? I miss both Mother and Dad so much, but I'm scared they will take you and Mystic away from me. Maybe Johnny has called Dad already. I hope so. He promised not to tell them where we are," Christy said, as she rubbed the filly's fuzzy neck and held Victoree's head close to her.

Johnny and Marlene had returned to the ranch house. Christy had promised to be there shortly, but she did want to spend a little more time with her Arabian horses. She knew it would be awkward and questions would be asked.

"I wish I could lie down in here with you two and just sleep," Christy said, as she continued to pet the mare and filly.

"Christy, are you in here?" came a voice from the barn door.

"I'm in Victoree's stall. I'm coming in just a minute," Christy answered.

The stall door opened, and Michael stepped inside.

"Dad said you spend almost all of your time here in the barn. He sent me down to tell you that lunch is ready," Michael said.

"I'm sorry. I guess I didn't realize how long it had been," Christy answered.

She felt somewhat self-conscious and didn't know what else to say. She quickly turned her head and felt her face flush. *What's wrong with me,* she thought. *I've been around boys before.*

"That's okay," Michael said, as he held the stall door open for her. "We better get going."

Their steps made a crunching sound in the frozen snow as the two teenagers walked toward the house. The cold air felt good on Christy's hot cheeks.

"Mom and Dad told us kids a little about your time in the mountains. That must have been something," Michael said, breaking the silence. "Maybe you can tell me all about it sometime."

"Sure," Christy replied, trying to sound nonchalant. "Anytime."

"So you are from Minnesota," Michael continued, as he kicked a rock from the pathway. "We went there once. My uncle and aunt used to live near Winona. They moved back here—must have been three or four years ago, so we never went back. It's pretty nice, but I like the mountains, especially here at the ranch. You should see it in the summertime. I can't think of any place I would rather be."

"It's beautiful now. I love the mountains too. I can see why you want to stay," Christy answered. She felt a small sense of joy and tranquillity. But now, now they were at the ranch house door. She dreaded going inside.

42

"There you are," Johnny said, as Christy and Michael entered the room. "Hurry and wash up. Ella is about to put lunch on the table."

"I'm sorry I'm late," Christy answered. "I'll hurry."

"I haven't called your parents yet, Christy," Johnny said, after they were seated at the table. "I wanted you to be here to hear the conversation. I won't break my promise and tell them where you are. Just let them know you are all right."

"Don't worry, Christy," Marlene added. "You don't need to talk to them until you are ready. Both Johnny and I felt you should hear what is said."

"That's okay. I would talk to them now if Mystic could travel that far. I know they'll come for me right away," Christy answered.

"We understand," Marlene responded.

Johnny finished eating. He picked up the cordless phone and dialed the number.

"Hello. Is this Dr. Baldwin?" Johnny asked.

Christy's eyes focused on her plate. She felt that everyone in the room was watching her. Even Mickey sat very still.

"I have news of your daughter. She is okay and will be calling you soon," Johnny said. "No, no. I'm not after your reward. I know. No, she is here with me and my family. She's doing fine and she will call you. No. I wish I could. Her horse is pretty sick, but she will be okay. Dr. Baldwin, I promised your daughter I would let you know she is okay. We know you must be sick with worry. I can't. I promised her she could tell you when she is ready. She's had a pretty terrifying experience. I can't tell you that. I wish I could, Dr. Baldwin. I know. You can trust me. She is okay. She'll call you, I promise," Johnny continued. "Mrs. Baldwin, your daughter is fine. She'll be calling. . . ."

Christy jumped up from the table and ran to Johnny.

"Let me talk to them. I'll talk to them now," Christy cried, tears streaming down the girl's pretty face.

Johnny smiled as he handed the phone to Christy.

"Hello, Dad. Mother, are you there too?" Christy asked. "I'm okay. No, they have been real nice to me. I'm okay, Mother. Victoree almost died. No. She's better now. We are in Montana. I'll tell you all about it. Dad, please don't take Victoree away from me. She already has. A little filly."

"You talk as long as you want to," Johnny said, as he patted Christy on the arm. "We'll go in the other room."

Johnny put his arm around his wife's shoulders as they left the kitchen.

"Did you take a course in psychology?" he whispered. "How did you know she would talk if she listened to my conversation?"

12
9
6
J. FLAGG

Marlene just smiled.

"They are flying here tomorrow," Christy all but shouted as she rushed into to the room. "Here, can you tell Dad where to fly to and how to get there? They are still on the phone."

"Yes, Dr. Baldwin. Northwest flies to Billings, Montana. I think Delta does too. Yes, there's rental cars there. We'll meet you at the airport. Call back when you've got your reservations made. It's no problem. We're on a ranch about eighty-five miles from Billings. It would be hard for you to find. We'll meet you. Okay, talk to you shortly," Johnny gave them the telephone number and hung up the phone.

"They aren't going to take Victoree away from me. I told them how she saved my life so many times. I don't have to go to Boston to school. They just want me to come home and be with them," Christy beamed. "They're not even mad at me. I can't wait to see them."

"That's wonderful, Christy. I am sure they are as happy as you are," Marlene said as she watched the young girl grab her jacket and rush out the door.

"I have to go tell Victoree," Christy shouted. "Oh, if Mother and Dad call before I get back in, will you tell them to bring me some clothes?"

Christy ran to the barn and was breathless as she hurried into Victoree's stall.

"We're going home, pretty girl. As soon as Mystic can travel, we're going home."

Christy threw her arms around the mare's neck. Mystic jumped to her feet and hid behind Victoree. Christy reached around the mare to pet the filly.

"I'm sorry I scared you, special baby," Christy said. "We're going home. Someday we'll come back. Maybe I can help Johnny some summer. He said I could. But now, now I just want to go home."